SEA GLASS AND SECOND CHANCES

CAROLINA COVE
BOOK 3

KAY LYONS

KINDRED SPIRITS PUBLISHING

So there you have it, New York. I'm Devon and that's *What's Hot.*" Devon Teeks held her smile until she received the all clear and then sank back into the uncomfortable chair on set. The splashy designer furniture might look fantastic on camera, but it was as comfortable as sitting on a rock.

"Devon, you said to remind you to leave *on time.*"

Devon blinked, her mind drawing blank.

"Your dinner with Mr. Up-and-Coming President?" her assistant, Tia, said. "Your anniversary?"

Devon stared at the twenty-something intern, fresh off the plane from Missouri and starry-eyed, just like Devon had been at the same age when she'd moved to New York City to intern at the station. "Of course. Thanks. I'm on my way."

She left the host's chair and moved off the dais toward the darkened area behind the cameras leading to the hallway and beyond. The greenroom was closest to the set, with her dressing room in a more private area toward the rear.

Halfway down the hallway, Devon paused to remove one of her ridiculously high heels and sighed when the cold floor tile seeped into her aching foot.

Had she really reached the age where she wanted comfort over looks? Didn't that make her *old*?

Giving in with a silent whimper, she removed the other heel and hurried along, reminding herself that it was the price to pay for going barefoot on Carolina Cove's sandy beaches the first twenty-five years of her life.

It wasn't until she moved to New York from the Wilmington, North Carolina, area that she realized just how casually she'd dressed. But in a tourist town, on an island no less, even newbie journalists couldn't fight the ninety-degree days and humidity of summer in the south.

She entered her dressing room and quickly showered off the heavy makeup, then redid her face and changed into the A-line bombshell dress Ted loved. The dress hugged every line and curve but was modest and sophisticated, with a zipper that ran full-length down her back that drew attention to her behind and all the squats she hated but did anyway.

Frowning at the shoes she'd chosen to go with the dress, she donned the ankle-strapped platform heels, grateful they lent a little more support to her achy feet. Finally ready, she grabbed her bag and belongings and headed out the door.

Ted had asked for her to clear her schedule tonight so they could spend some time together. They'd been working too many hours lately, and the stress they both carried from their jobs had started to intrude on their relationship. They got along great face-to-face, but when their schedules kept them apart, they wound up bickering over silly things.

But seeing as it was their one-year anniversary, tonight would be different. They'd block out the world, set all the stress and issues aside, relax, and be together.

Devon donned her oversized sunglasses as she left the building, smiling at her driver as he greeted her and opened the door of the black town car provided by the network to ensure their on-screen hosts arrived on time. "How are you today, Tony?"

"Ah, can't complain, Miss Devon. Things go well for you?"

"Perfectly." They had the same conversation every day, and today was no different—until John Prescott came rushing out of the building calling her name and asking her to wait.

"Stay or go?" Tony asked quickly.

"Stay," she said with a glance at her watch.

She tossed her belongings into the back of the car and turned to see John skid to a halt a foot away.

"Devon, I'm glad I caught you. We need to talk," John said, breathing heavily from the rush.

"Whatever it is, it has to wait. I can't tonight."

"You said that last night."

"Because *you* insisted I go to that gala even though I had to get up at four a.m. to fill in on the morning show before taping my own."

"Your schedule is open this evening."

"No, it isn't," she said firmly. "I have plans."

"Well, this can't wait," John said. "I'm afraid I have bad news."

"Not now, John. Please."

"You know your ratings are down," he continued without pause, "and the network... they've decided to cancel the show. Today was the last taping."

The air left her lungs in a rush and she gaped at

him. "*What*? How is that possible? They can't just... Can't we at least finish the season?"

John held up his hands. "I'm sorry. I'm not happy about it either. But they say we're done so... we're done. Don't bother coming in tomorrow unless it's to gather your stuff and take it to the morning show so it'll be there when you start."

She blinked at him, certain she'd misheard him. "I'm sorry, what?"

John's ruddy face broke out in a grin and he chuckled. "Congratulations. You got the fill-in position. Natalie officially goes on maternity leave next week, which means you get a week to make getting up before dawn a habit. It's been wonderful working with you. Congratulations."

John held out his hand and she shook it, a huff of a laugh leaving her chest before she stepped toward him and gave him a quick hug. Maybe she'd lost the gig she presented daily, but the morning host position would give her time to secure something else. "Thank you. It's been wonderful working with you. I've learned so much."

"Knock 'em dead, kid. And enjoy your week off."

A week off? What would she do with a whole week off?

She didn't remember having a week off since

moving to the city ten years ago. After all, when you were trying to climb the network's ladder, time off didn't exist. She'd worked her job, filled in on others, volunteered, whatever it took, going above and beyond in order to move up the ranks. Her reputation as being reliable and there no matter what had given her ins with the network she didn't take for granted.

But a week... Maybe she and Ted could get away for a few days?

"Ms. Devon? Everything okay?" Tony asked.

A laugh rumbled out of her. "Yeah, it is. Surprisingly so. I just lost *and* landed a great position, and today is my anniversary."

"Well, now. Let's get you home so you can celebrate," Tony said.

From inside the car, Devon watched John's return to the building, her stomach fluttering with excitement.

The ride to her tiny apartment took a ridiculous amount of time considering the distance. She stared out the window at the crowded streets unseeing because her mind raced with ideas and plans and things to be done.

She had a feeling Ted was going to broach the subject of her moving in with him again tonight, but she'd promised herself from a very young age she would always have a place to go home to unless there was a wedding ring on her finger. Breakups happened. She'd watched it happen too many times to otherwise smart women who found themselves homeless and surfing friends' couches until they made other arrangements. She wouldn't be one of them.

They arrived at her building, and she flashed a smile at the doorman when he opened the car door.

"Good evening, ma'am. Mr. George arrived thirty minutes ago and is waiting upstairs."

"Thank you."

Devon said goodbye to Tony and made her way inside the building. The beautiful lobby was decorated in black-and-white checkerboard tile polished to a high gleam. The seating area on the right looked elegant yet sturdy, the red leather couch, matching chairs, and dark wood coffee table drawing the eye.

Devon bypassed the seating, greeted the ever-present and familiar security guard behind his shiny wooden desk, and punched the elevator button. The large doors opened in an instant.

The move to this building had taken place several years ago when she'd finally received a promotion, including a much-needed raise that allowed her to get her own place. While small, the apartment provided security and was more convenient to the network's location.

Once the elevator was in motion, she glanced at her reflection in the polished metal and sighed. Even that distorted image looked tired, but when she'd burned the candle at both ends for the last ten years, how could she not?

Maybe a vacation to somewhere tropical was just what she needed to celebrate? Could she convince Ted to leave his office for a few days and go?

Ratings for *What's Hot* had been down for a while. Those in the know didn't watch the show to find out the latest clubs or restaurants, plays. No, social media filled them in.

The generations that watched were the "oldies" and more apt to be retiring and moving out of the bustling city than clubbing the night away.

With any luck, maybe the host she temporarily replaced on the morning show would decide not to come back to work? Want to spend more time with her newborn?

The elevator doors opened, and she made her way down the hall, staring at the patterned carpet beneath her feet. The door was unlocked and she entered with a chipper hello.

She glanced around but didn't see him. "Ted? I have news!"

"Coming," he called.

Seconds later, Theodore Carlton George III appeared from the bathroom still straightening his tie. Ted smiled as he crossed the room and kissed her on her cheek.

"Look at you. My favorite dress."

"I thought you'd like it."

"You know I do. You look amazing, as always. What's this about news? Does this have anything to do with a certain morning news anchor position?"

"How did you know?" she asked, her excitement deflating a bit.

"I may have heard some rumblings about your show ending and... put in a good word for you."

Wait, what? So she hadn't gotten the position on her own but because of her relationship with Ted and his political future?

"Come on, don't look like that. All that's important is that you got the job, right?"

"Yes, but I thought I'd gotten it on my own."

"You did," Ted told her. "All I did was make a few calls. You can't be upset with me for that, now can you? Let's celebrate. I'll pop the champagne."

She watched as he moved toward the kitchen and forced herself to shrug off her upset.

She was very familiar with the red tape surrounding promotions within the network. And unlike others, she had no deep contacts or connections within the company, so she told herself to be grateful Ted had been willing to make the calls on her behalf. "You're right. Thank you for doing whatever you did."

"I just made it clear you'd be interested and that it would be a personal favor if they gave you a chance. You did the work, Devon."

She had—though the way he'd stated it, he had not only pulled strings but tied them in a knot by connecting it with his political future. She didn't like it—but she also couldn't argue the doing since it was done.

"Come on. Don't be upset with me. If I was up for a job and you could say something to help me, wouldn't you do the same?"

She would. And when he put it like that... she felt petty being upset by what he'd done for her. "I would. Thank you," she said again.

"You're welcome. Now let's celebrate."

"Well, if you'd *really* like to celebrate, I have a few ideas."

"Is that right?"

"As of today, I have a week's vacation. I thought maybe we could take a trip? Just the two of us? Maybe go somewhere tropical?" she asked hopefully. With his schedule, it would be much more difficult for him to get away, but she hoped to convince him all the same. "Sugar-white sand? Umbrellas in our drinks? Steel drum music floating in the air?"

"That sounds fantastic, but you know I can't be away from the city right now. Not with an election coming up in a few months."

"I knew you'd say that," she said with a playful pout. "But I had to ask."

"One day, sweetheart. And until then, I know of a special way we can celebrate," he said.

"How?"

"Like this," he said, moving toward her and getting down on one knee. "Devon Teeks, will you do me the honor of marrying me?"

RAYNA JO TEEKS watched the online feed of Devon's *What's Hot* the moment she was able to and frowned at her daughter's image. Devon looked tired. And much too thin.

Like any mother, she worried about Devon's health and whether or not New York was actually good for her. She seemed to always be on the go, never resting, rarely calling.

"How's one of my favorite nieces?" Adaline asked.

Rayna Jo glanced at her twin, frown still in place. "She looks exhausted."

"Lots to do in that city," Adaline said in a distracted tone.

Her sixty-three-year-old sister put the finishing touches on a sample display board, noting the masculine colors and theme. "Who's that for?" Rayna Jo asked.

Adaline's face filled with color, and Rayna Jo felt her stomach clench in unease. "Is that for the man who came in last week? Dan or Dean—"

"As a matter of fact, it is. *Dale* has returned a time or two since and asked if I would handle his account personally."

"Oh, Adaline. Is that wise? He flirted awfully hard with you."

Adaline's color increased still more, and she lifted her perfectly manicured left hand and the wide gold band she wore. "He's well aware I'm married."

"That certainly didn't seem to stop him," Rayna Jo murmured, unable to keep the note of disapproval from her tone.

"Why should it? Flirting *means* nothing."

"Flirting eventually leads to more," Rayna Jo said. "Addy—"

"Don't Addy me. It's *fine*. You're overreacting and worrying about nothing. What's the harm in a few smiles and winks?"

"The harm is that you're a *married* woman, and he isn't your husband."

"So we've established. Ray-Ray, stop being so naive. It's totally innocent. Besides, I can't say as I mind getting a few compliments. Hugh's as flirtatious as a rock. *On the bottom of the ocean.* I don't know that he's even paid me a compliment these past *ten* years."

"Hugh is a gem," Rayna Jo argued. "Maybe he's not as outgoing and romantic as you'd like, but he's a good, solid man who worships the ground you walk on. Don't take that for granted."

Adaline pursed her lips and shot Rayna Jo a look from beneath her lashes. "I'm not."

"You *are*. You're playing with fire and think no one will get burned."

"I'm adding spice to a pot that hasn't simmered

in a long, *long* time. Do you think Richard goes on all his business trips and *never* turns his head when a pretty woman walks by?"

No, she was sure her husband *did* turn his head. And a lot more. But it didn't make it right. Nor did it make the awareness of his actions and behavior hurt any less. "What's innocent to you might not be considered innocent to what's-his-name."

"*Dale*. And you worry entirely too much," Adaline said, pinning the last of the navy-and-white-striped fabric to the board. "There. What do you think?"

The board was as gorgeous as they always were when Adaline prepped them. She had a keen decorating eye and used fabrics and textures some might not think would work together.

The board she'd created made for a unique and fabulously understated nautical look well suited for a rich bachelor in a beach town. "When is his appointment?"

She'd hoped to get home early tonight because, unlike her sister, she *felt* her age. Plus, she liked to look her best when Richard returned from one of his trips, and if she could squeeze in a nap, the beauty sleep couldn't hurt.

"I'm meeting Dale at his house," Adaline said,

avoiding Rayna Jo's gaze. "Speaking of which, I'd better get a move on or I'll be late."

"I'll come with you," Rayna Jo said. "We've been slow all day today. It wouldn't hurt to close up a bit early."

"No need," Adaline said, picking up the board after getting her purse from small storage area behind the cash register. "Go home. I'll see you tomorrow."

Rayna Jo watched as Adaline hurried out the door, heart heavy with the danger ahead for her sister. Maybe Addy could stay strong in the face of the client's flirting, but why take the risk? Why put herself in the position to teeter on a line that shouldn't be crossed? How would Hubert feel if he knew?

If Adaline was so unhappy with her marriage, why not go to counseling? Do whatever she could to get the spark back? Anything but seek attention elsewhere.

Rayna Jo left the check-out area and moved through the empty design and decor store, watching as Adaline loaded the board into the back of her Range Rover and shot out of the parking lot.

Adaline's comment about Richard's behavior on his business trips had struck a chord, and now she couldn't shake the dark thoughts or the pain Adaline had inadvertently caused.

She knew very well what took place while her husband was away. Every now and again, she'd see Richard's receipts. Dinner for two. Drinks. Charges from female clothing stores, lingerie stores that never ended up as gifts for her. Orders for flowers she didn't receive. Room service for two.

Funny how some men could be so charming and romantic before marriage, but afterwards, the only women they romanced were the ones who didn't wear their ring.

Her stomach knotted as it always did when she thought of her forty-two-year marriage.

By all accounts, she and Richard had it all. A big, gorgeous house facing the Atlantic, two beautiful twin daughters, each successful in her own right. Nice cars. Great friends.

But peel back the layers, and for the last twenty years, it had all been a sham. She hated the deception of it. Hated that they played the part of the happy couple because... well, for her it was simply easier than facing the truth and starting over.

And for Richard, though they'd never truly discussed it, she believed he liked the convenience of having his cake and eating it, too. She was well aware that, for men like Richard, it was safer to have a wife. After all, it kept pesky mistresses in their place and the relationship between them exactly what it was —physical.

Still, it wasn't like she hadn't ever considered putting an end to the shenanigans. But then what? She was sixty-three. Her life almost over.

It was far too late to find her happily ever after....

CHAPTER TWO

Five minutes after her arrival home, Devon's head whirled. First the job—regardless of how it had come about—and now a proposal?

"Should I take your speechlessness as a yes?" he asked, sliding a gorgeous, cushion-cut diamond from a tiny blue box.

"Oh, of course! Yes!"

Grinning, he slid it onto her finger, kissed her hand, and rose to his feet, drawing her closer while lowering his head for a kiss.

Devon closed her eyes and smiled against Ted's lips.

A bell dinged.

Devon drew back with a small groan and heard

her cell phone ding again. "I'm sorry. I forgot to turn it off."

Ted kissed her again but released her when it sounded a third time. She bent to find the phone in her purse. "There," she said, silencing the call without looking at the caller ID.

Devon tossed the phone back into her bag, but within a few seconds, it began buzzing again. "Well, someone is persistent."

"Answer it," Ted said, "while I open the bottle and get the celebration going."

Devon pulled her phone out of her bag just as it began to buzz a fourth time. She frowned at the screen, seeing her twin sister's name. "Hey, Dara. Now's not a good time. You'll never guess—"

"I texted you an address," her sister said, cutting Devon off. "A helicopter will pick you up from there in forty-five minutes."

"What? What are you talking about?" Devon asked.

"Dad's been in an accident," Dara said, sounding rushed as she spoke. "He's critical and in transport to the hospital. It's bad, Dev. *Really* bad. The woman he was with died at the scene. I'm working out of town but heading out now to meet up with you.

We're taking the Guardian Group jet so we can get to Wilmington faster."

"Wait, *what?* Stand still, you're moving around so much I can't understand you," she said, meeting Ted's gaze from across the room. "Did you say... What do you mean, *the woman he was with?*"

The noise on the other end stopped, indicating Dara had taken Devon's advice to stop moving. Still, the emotion in Dara's voice grabbed hold of Devon and rocked her to her core.

"Dev, Dad was caught—*literally*—with his pants down. The woman... well, while he was driving."

"*What?*"

"Dad lost control and hit a vehicle head-on. Inside was freaking Oliver Beck, of all people."

Devon sucked in a sharp breath. "The *actor?*"

"Yes! He'd just left a fundraising event and was in full view of the media when it happened, and Mom is about to find out all the gory details."

"How do *you* know the gory details?" she said, struggling to focus with the onslaught of information and TMI she'd just received.

"Because one of our former guards is now Oliver's head of security and was driving. He's fine, but when he got to Dad and pulled his ID, he recognized the name and remembered I'm from the area, so he called me at the scene."

Devon couldn't process the details fast enough. This couldn't be happening. "What does Mom know?"

"Only that Dad was in an accident. Look, I've already contacted the Babes and asked them to isolate Mom until we get there, but the reality is she could see or hear something at any moment. Get your stuff and be at the address I texted you. I'll meet you in DC, and we'll go to Wilmington from there."

"I-I... Of course."

The phone clicked in her ear and Devon's knees buckled beneath her. She sank onto the edge of the couch, nauseous and wanting to hurl whatever might be in her empty stomach.

"That sounded ominous," Ted said, looking concerned as he made his way back to her side. "What's going on?"

She closed her eyes and repeated what Dara had told her. "My poor mom. I can't even imagine... I have to go pack."

"What? No. Devon, you can't be anywhere near that mess."

She blinked at him, her thoughts racing too fast

to focus even while going over everything Dara had just told her. "What?"

"Sweetheart, you're not thinking clearly. You know I'm right. Text Dara back and tell her to go without you."

"Absolutely not!"

"Devon—"

"My dad is critical a-and the woman in his car *died*. My mom—"

"Has her sister and friends and your sister to help her cope. You get involved and you will create an even bigger media storm than there already is because of him hitting Oliver Beck."

She shoved herself off the couch and paced across the floor to stare out at the street. The sun had fallen and lights glittered, traffic buzzed with typical fervor, and Ted's reflection in the window behind her left Devon feeling shredded—and selfish.

Why couldn't she have had one day to enjoy the moment? An evening to celebrate? "I know it's going to be a mess," she said, turning to face him, "but I have to go."

"I'm telling you to stay."

She gaped at him, blinking twice before finding her voice. "You're *telling* me?"

He had the grace to look embarrassed by his

choice of words. "Begging? Whatever the word, I am. Devon, please, don't get mixed up in that publicity nightmare."

"I'm certainly not happy about the circumstances, but he's still my *father*. Ted, my mom will need all the support she can get when she finds out about this. And God forbid, but what if Dad doesn't make it?"

"You can still be there for her. For them both. Call, video chat, *text*. But don't screw up your career and all your hard work by getting linked with that."

"I'm already linked," she said, incredulous at his response. "You know it's only a matter of time before my name is out there. Dara is stopped all the time by people thinking she's me. Even if I'm not there, the connection is."

Ted wiped a hand roughly over his face. "You would have to have an identical twin. For the love of... What a disaster."

"Yes, well, surely you realize my mother is the one suffering the worst? We're just snow in the avalanche."

Ted shook his head, muttered a curse, and stalked across the room, not stopping until he stood toe-to-toe with her.

"Devon, I know you're hurting and scared, but this impacts me, too."

"I know," she said softly, regretfully. "I'm sorry. I really am. I know how hard you've worked to steer clear of any sort of scandal, but it's not like I had or have a say in this."

"But you do."

"I don't!"

He ran both hands over his hair in frustration, mussing his otherwise perfect look.

Ted was a handsome man. A Kennedy-esque golden boy who'd quickly moved up the city's political tiers. Next stop, state senator. Then on to more—if he kept his golden boy image.

"This certainly isn't how I thought tonight would end."

"I'm sure it wasn't the way my father and mother thought things would go for them either," she said dryly.

Usually Ted was good-natured. Kind. Smiling. Willing to jump in and help any good cause.

But now he looked perturbed and annoyed, and there wasn't much she could do about it without betraying her family in the process. "Ted, instead of avoiding this, why don't you come with me? Show your support as my... fiancé?" she said, holding up her hand and the stunningly beautiful ring. "I'd love to be able to officially introduce you to my family. We've certainly waited long enough. They ask about you in every conversation."

"I don't think that's a good idea."

She hated that their night had been ruined. Hated what she saw happening. Did he regret asking her to marry him? "It's our anniversary. We just got *engaged*! Please, come with me. If something happens to my dad... I'd like it if you were there for me."

"I want to be there for you, too, Devon. I do, but you know how tricky this could get for me."

Ted inhaled and rubbed a hand across his face again, and she watched, waiting for him to decide.

"I'm sorry. I can't leave the city right now. There's just too much going on. You go, and I'll stay here and do what damage control I can."

She crossed her arms over her front and squeezed. As a solution, it was okay, but she couldn't help but wonder... "So that's all we are? Publicity and image?"

He framed her face with his palms and kissed her forehead before brushing his lips across hers.

"Of course not. But my calendar is packed with meetings I already rescheduled in order to be with you tonight. Go if you insist," he said, thumb brushing just under her lip. "But go knowing this could change things for you."

"What do you mean?"

"Devon, with all the reports of sexual misconduct and story accuracy, networks want their anchors squeaky clean. Your involvement could negatively influence your job prospects."

The statement caused her stomach to knot up even more. "I hadn't thought of that."

"You should."

She closed her eyes and squeezed them tight. Why did everything have to be so complicated?

"My advice to you is to send flowers, call your mom, and stay low until this blows over and you can visit without adding fuel to the fire."

She fisted her hands, engagement ring forgotten. "What if I can't *do* that?"

"You can—you just don't want to."

She held up her hand. "What about this?"

"What about it?"

"Would you...like it back?"

OSCAR ROMAN WATCHED as his best friend heeded his doctor brother's advice and avoided the press-crowded emergency room entrance. Michael drove around the hospital and parked, and they hurried toward a side entrance Michael's twin had told them to use.

Inside, Oz walked beside his best friend since childhood, their fast strides eating up the distance to the desk that could point them in the right direction.

The woman behind the desk asked a security guard to take them to a waiting area, and once they arrived, Oz's gaze fastened on the group of people clustered around Rayna Jo Teeks.

His heart pinched at the sight. He couldn't imagine the pain she must be suffering, and yet she didn't even know the worst of it.

Oz had been hanging out with Michael and procrastinating on his latest book when Michael's cousin Dara had texted out an alert to immediately isolate her mother and why.

Thanks to some quick maneuvering, the woman's friends had gotten Rayna Jo to the hospital and into a waiting area with no television to try to spare her the salacious details of her husband's behavior at the time of the accident.

On the way to the hospital, a local radio station

jockey was already reporting the circumstances of Richard Teeks's accident due to a passerby snapping a photo or two and actually *posting* them on the internet. The DJ was having a field day cracking jokes, despite the fact a woman had died and Richard Teeks was in critical condition.

It was bad enough to deal with the news of the accident and her husband's touch-and-go status, but top it off with an affair and details about the crash?

Rayna Jo, Dara, and Devon didn't deserve that.

"We came as soon as we heard," Michael said to his aunt.

Once Michael hugged Rayna Jo and moved out of the way, Oz greeted the woman with a kiss on her soft cheek, noting how much Rayna Jo had aged since he'd last seen her.

"Thank you for coming," Rayna Jo whispered, the words choked with tears. "All of you... I appreciate it so much, but there's no need for everyone to be here and wait with me. I'll be fine. The girls will arrive soon."

"We're not leaving you," Mary Elizabeth Shipley said.

Feeling more than a little awkward and helpless, Oz took a step back to simply observe the Babes.

The lifelong friends surrounded Rayna Jo with

their love and support, their loyalty sweet and sincere.

Having grown up down the street from Michael and his identical twin brother, Logan, Oz knew the story of how the Babes' friendships came about.

During the summers of '58 and '59, four of the prominent Carolina Cove neighbors and friends had given birth to baby girls. One a set of twins—Rayna Jo and Adaline.

The proud mamas had taken the girls for daily strolls in their prams—and the locals had nicknamed the group the Boardwalk Babes—a name used to this day by the five sixty-somethings.

All in all, the group consisted of the five Babes, who'd had twelve children between them, with Rayna Jo and Adeline each having a set of twins. On top of the second generation, a third had started, with Cheryl Dummit and Mary Elizabeth having grandchildren.

"The girls will be here soon," Rayna Jo said again. Comforting herself?

As though summoned by the statement, the automatic doors of the hospital parted with a whoosh of air, and Oz's stomach dropped to the floor until he realized the woman walking in wasn't Devon.

Dara and Devon were Rayna Jo's identical twins

but as different as night and day despite their physical similarities. They both had the same sandy-blond hair and features, but Dara was typically dressed casually, in comfortable clothing for her long hours behind a screen as a cybersecurity specialist, while Devon sported a more feminine look, her profession requiring her to always be made up and camera ready.

Dara met Oz's gaze with one of pity because she no doubt knew what he went through each time he saw her, and he acknowledged her glance with a small nod. Dara's gaze shifted to the crowd and she rushed to her mother.

"Hey, Mama. How are you?" Dara asked.

"Oh, Dara, I'm... How did you get here so quickly?" Rayna Jo asked.

"One of the perks of being a good employee. My boss let us use the private plane. How's Dad?" Dara asked with a glance at those gathered.

"He's still in surgery," Adaline said, patting her sister's hand. "The nurse said it could be several more hours."

"I just don't understand. Your father said he was going to be in Cincinnati two more days," Rayna Jo said. "Why didn't he tell me he was home?"

Oz's heart broke for the woman, especially in light of the answer to that question.

The doors whooshed open again, and he knew before he turned who it was. His pulse picked up speed, and he braced himself before shifting his attention to Devon.

She was as beautiful as always, though looking more tired and stressed than he ever remembered her being. She wore it in the stiff way she moved and her drawn features.

"Hey, Mama."

"Devon, oh, my babies, I'm so glad you're both here," Rayna Jo said, tugging her daughters close for a long hug.

The woman's sobs filled the waiting area, and it was quite some time before Rayna Jo managed to gather her emotions.

The waiting game continued another hour, with everyone speaking in whispers and being very careful of what they said in front of Rayna Jo.

She'd have to be told, but how did one pick a good time to hear such news? Especially while waiting to see if her husband survived surgery.

"Mrs. Teeks?" a man said.

Oz looked up and blinked, not expecting to see a Hollywood superstar or the hulking guard at his side, along with a curly-haired woman who also looked vaguely familiar and another woman as well.

"Oh. Oh, Mr. Beck, I'm so sorry," Rayna Jo said to the man.

"Don't get up," Oliver Beck said when Rayna Jo began to do just that. "We just wanted to stop in and check on you."

"That's very kind of you. It's s-so good to see you up and about. You're okay? Truly?" Rayna Jo asked.

"I'm fine, ma'am. Just some cuts and bruises, nothing serious," Oliver said. "Denz, here, took the brunt of it," he said, indicating the bodyguard. "And he was still able to get out and walk away with the same. Our wives are here to see us home."

Oz's brain finally did some connecting on its own, and he remembered that Beck had married a local woman, a professional matchmaker, no less. He'd seen her picture in the tabloids, on the news, and online, and that's why she looked so familiar.

Oz watched as Dara backed up and discreetly moved over to where Oliver's guard stood. The two began a private conversation, confirming what Michael had told him about how Dara had come to know the intimate details of the accident and was able to alert them in order to protect Rayna Jo.

Both looked grim when Dara slowly made her way back toward her mom.

"Mr. Beck, I'm Dara Teeks. Denz told you that I work for Guardian Group?"

"Yes, he did," Oliver said. "I'm glad he was able to contact you after the accident," Oliver said carefully.

"Me, too. I just wanted to add my apologies and express my relief that you're okay."

Rayna Jo's eyes filled with tears that trickled down her cheeks. "I-I'm sure my husband will want to apologize the moment he wakes up from surgery. He's never had an accident before. He's normally such a good driver."

"No worries, ma'am. But I do hope someone will keep me posted on his condition," he said, glancing at Dara, who nodded.

"Of course, Mr. Beck."

"Please know we'll be praying for your husband and family, Mrs. Teeks," Beck's wife said.

"Thank you. And I, you," Rayna Jo said.

Throughout the exchange, Devon had remained quiet, but as Oliver Beck turned to walk away, he caught sight of her and stopped.

The man then glanced from Devon to Dara and back to Devon again, and from across the room, Oz could see the man's brain cranking as he put the pieces together.

"Devon...from *What's Hot?*" Oliver asked.

Devon looked like she wanted to crawl under the nearby chairs, but instead she moved toward Beck and held out her hand. "It's nice to see you again, Mr. Beck. We met on the red carpet two years ago after you filmed *Moonshadow*."

"I thought you looked familiar," he said, tilting his head at Dara. "I didn't realize you had a twin."

"I try to stay *out* of the spotlight as much as possible," Dara said with a small smile. "She's in it enough for both of us."

Oliver Beck chuckled at the statement and nodded. "I understand that. Well, I'll leave you to comfort your mother. Please keep me informed."

"Yessir," Dara said.

The moment Oliver Beck and the others left the waiting area, everyone kind of looked at each other in astonishment. The night just kept getting weirder and weirder.

Lights flashed outside the windows, and Oz realized they were camera lights taking photos of Oliver leaving the hospital.

"Mom, we need to talk to you," Dara said with a glance at her sister. "About the accident and... Dad."

"What about it?" Rayna Jo asked.

"Dara, dear," Tessa Gallagher, another of the Babes, said, "why don't you and Devon go get us all some coffee? Let us Babes handle things here for a bit."

Tessa gave Rayna Jo's daughters a firm nod before she tilted her head toward the door.

"That's a good idea. It might be a little easier coming from us than from you, hon," Mary Elizabeth added.

"What might be easier? What do you mean?" Rayna Jo asked. "What are you not telling me?"

Adaline took hold of her sister's hand and squeezed.

"It's all right," Adaline said to Rayna Jo. To the rest of them, she said, "If you're not a Babe, go get some coffee. Ray-Ray and I'll take a mocha on your way back."

One by one, those gathered filed out of the room. The Babes' husbands who were present were the first to bolt as quickly as they could, with Michael catching up with his dad to speak to him. Dara and Devon were next, and Oz brought up the rear.

"This is not okay," Dara muttered. "Mom is going to be devastated when she hears the details."

"She will be. But her friends and family will help

her pick up the pieces," Oz said softly, watching as Dara glanced over her shoulder toward him while Devon purposely kept her gaze ahead of her. "Just like y'all did for me," he continued, "when Devon left me at the altar."

CHAPTER THREE

Devon ignored Oz's comment and marched onward, determined to be the first to down some hopefully decent coffee and try to pretend she was perfectly capable of handling everything getting thrown at her.

Besides, she hadn't left him *at* the altar but called things off before—well, packing her bags and leaving to escape the upset she'd caused by calling off the wedding with only days to spare.

She couldn't even be surprised that Oz was there, because he had always been an extension of the family.

Her first love had grown up down the street, an only child who'd joined the gang of cousins playing in yards and on the boardwalk, drawn to the noise and fun and snacks from the Babes.

It wasn't long before Oz stayed for meals and attended special gatherings, accompanied them on campouts, and went on vacations with them since he was best friends with her cousin Michael.

After Oz's mother had died of cancer, the Babes had done all they could to help Oz's single father cope by both feeding them and taking Oz off the man's hands as much as possible.

But between Devon's late-night gala and early-morning recordings, the shock of the accident, and now this?

Her energy level dragged, and her emotions were as fried as most everything was in the south. Then burnt to a crisp just for kicks.

Ted had refused her offer to take the ring back, and while that in and of itself should have relieved some of her anxiety about the situation, something in his expression hadn't helped.

Ted had given her a sad, slightly frustrated stare, curled her fingers with his, and lifted her hand for a kiss.

Then the apartment door had shut softly behind him as he left without another word.

Now she wore the beautiful ring but wondered if

she was really engaged. Would tomorrow morning's headlines be the deciding factor for Ted?

The stress of her relationship added to the news of her father's accident and the conditions surrounding it, his critical condition, and she was just done for the day. The week. So very done.

The last thing she wanted was to have to answer questions she didn't have the answers to regarding her relationship with Ted.

"You can't just ignore him, you know," Dara said from behind her.

Devon discreetly slid the stone around her finger so that it didn't show. She stepped up to the all-night coffee and snack bar and ordered first, leaving the tab open for those behind her after sliding the barista enough cash to cover the drinks plus a generous tip. "I'm not ignoring anyone."

"Oh, really? How do you figure that?" Dara asked.

Devon shifted down the counter toward the pickup area. "Don't make this more difficult than it already is," she said as she passed Dara.

Dara huffed and, after she placed her order, moved to join Devon.

"It wouldn't be difficult at all if you'd just talk to him. Get rid of all the weirdness. It was ten *years* ago, and you were the one who broke things off. Isn't it time to apologize and put things behind you?"

"I have."

"Ohhh, no, you haven't," Dara argued. "You haven't settled anything, you've *avoided*. Him *and* us, if we're being completely honest."

Devon felt Oz's gaze on her from across the hospital's coffee shop and moved toward the windows.

Down below, a bevy of journalists waited like vultures, and she found herself embarrassed to be linked to the same profession. Journalists did plenty of good in the world. They exposed wrongs, revealed corruption, and highlighted the stories people needed to hear.

But some also exploited situations like this for the sensationalism and shock value with no thought or care given to the innocent family members hurt in the backlash and fallout.

She stood at the window, unable to believe the shocking details Dara had told her on the flight to Wilmington. Details her sister had gotten firsthand from Oliver Beck's bodyguard. She could only imagine what the man had thought when he'd found her father and the woman and realized what had happened.

"Your coffee," a low voice said from behind her.

She turned sideways and focused on the cup with her name on it, rather than the masculine hand holding it for the exchange.

"Devon, I'm sorry about what I said earlier. Now's not the time to delve into history. And seeing that it is old news, let's just put it behind us and move on. Water and bridge. Okay?"

The sound of Oz's deep southern drawl shredded what was left of her nerves. She inhaled in a sad attempt to brace herself for face-to-face contact, because after so many years, nothing had changed.

Oh, they had a few more wrinkles than when they were twenty-five and twenty-eight, but the hint of gray in Oz's dark hair made her pulse race. Almost-forty Oz was even more handsome. "Okay," she said finally. "I'd like that. It's been a difficult day."

"That it has. How are you holding up?" he asked.

She opened her mouth to speak only to close it again, unable to find the words to express herself with anything other than a shake of her head.

"Yeah, I get it. I'm sorry, sweetheart. None of you deserve this mess."

She ignored the term of endearment. *Sweetheart, honey,* and *darling* were as common in the south as expletives were elsewhere. "Did you know he was having an affair?" she asked. "I mean, I know how gossip works, especially when you live in a fishbowl."

It was one of the things she'd hated about the island. Probably the only thing she'd hated about it. But when there were only a few thousand full-time residents, it was inevitable that there would be gossip like any other small town.

Oz shook his head, one side of his lips twisting into a grimace.

"No. I'm as surprised as everyone else. Devon, look, I know things between us have been strained all of these years, but... Rayna Jo is going to need us, all of us, to get through this. I'd like to think nothing will keep you from reaching out to me if you need something."

She swallowed the lump in her throat and nodded. "Thank you."

Oz leaned a shoulder against the metal support between the giant windows of the hospital, his gaze raking over her features.

She fought the urge to duck her head, knowing she wasn't at her best.

"I hear you have your own show."

"Ah, well, had. It's been fun," she managed to say. "But it ended today."

"I'm sorry. I hadn't heard."

"It's all good. I've just been hired to temporarily co-host a morning show while I explore other options."

"Are you looking at anything in particular?" Oz asked.

He seemed interested but she knew it was a matter of being polite. Leave it to Oz to remember his manners at a time like this.

But like it or not, her attention shifted to the tiny platinum band she felt rubbing against the bottom of the coffee cup. "I haven't had much time to think about it."

"Well, good luck. Maybe you'll have more time to visit. I know your mom was happy to see you. Everyone is, including me."

She forced a smile and wrapped her other hand around the warm cup. The hospital was cold. Or maybe she was just chilled from the nerves and the grief and the horror of what her father had done and all the day had held.

"I hadn't heard. Congratulations."

Her gaze shot back to his and she watched as Oz stared at her hand. She quickly glanced around them and turned so that her back was to the group. "It's not—" She twisted it around to show him it was an engagement ring and not a wedding band. "Don't mention it, please. Now's not the time and... it's new and complicated."

She set the cup on the window ledge and was painfully aware of Oz's gaze on her while she discreetly slipped the ring off and tucked it into her pocket.

"So I see."

Yeah, she felt no awkwardness from the man she'd once been engaged to about the ring now tying her to someone else. "Look, Oz, I appreciate you coming over to talk, but I'm not really—"

A code blue was called for the surgical floor, and she felt like her heart stopped beating. Anger and adrenaline had kept her going until now, but her father was still her father, and she'd always been a daddy's girl.

Her gaze met Dara's across the room, and simultaneously the two of them bolted toward the door, leaving the others behind.

They raced back to the waiting area to find her mother sobbing in a chair, surrounded by the Babes. No one spoke as they waited on word.

Minutes stretched and finally a secured door opened. A grim-looking doctor in surgical scrubs emerged. Devon knew without being told what the outcome had been. The cold she'd felt before now spread to every part of her body.

"Mrs. Teeks?"

"Yes," Rayna Jo said, tears streaming. "How... How is he?"

"Mrs. Teeks, I'm Dr. Abbot. Your husband had a lot of internal bleeding and damage from the accident. We did everything we could, but your husband passed on the table. I'm very sorry for your loss."

Devon closed her eyes when her mother released a sobbing wail that tore at her very soul, the cry sounding like a wounded animal being tortured.

A hand touched her shoulder and gently squeezed, and Devon felt herself being turned and hugged against a strong male chest.

She breathed in Oz's scent but she didn't cry. Couldn't.

She was too angry. Too horrified that her father would always be remembered as the man who died *that* way. What was he thinking? Why had he done this? How could he?

"It's going to be okay."

Oz's softly whispered words brought out the tears she refused to shed for a man who would do this to his family. To his loving wife of *forty-two years.*

She swallowed hard and forced the tears away. "It's not," she said. "It's so *not* okay."

Oz didn't speak again. He just squeezed her tight and held her, and she was grateful for that support because, at the moment, she wasn't sure her legs would hold her.

This was why she'd wanted Ted here with her. This was what she'd feared.

And even though she told herself to extract herself from Oz and not give in to the need to be comforted, she couldn't force herself to move.

The whirl of multiple cameras sounded loudly in the room.

"Hey!"

Adam Shipley, Mary Elizabeth's husband, hurried after the photographers who'd managed to sneak into the hospital.

Devon stared in horror while the cameras continued to click, and just as Adam and Michael reached them, the men ran out the door.

And though she didn't say a word, everyone turned to look at them, and Devon realized, given their position, they would be very much front and center of the photographs depicting Richard Teeks's family.

She pushed Oz away, feeling sick to her stomach

and praying somehow her face hadn't been visible, and rushed to her mother, who sat sobbing.

"It can't be," Rayna Jo said. "It just can't *be*."

DEVON WAS EXHAUSTED by the time they got back to her parents' house situated along the Carolina Cove boardwalk.

She and Dara had rented a vehicle at the airport, but because of the reporters and their upset, Oz had volunteered to drive so that Devon, Dara, and their mother could sit in the back behind the darker-tinted windows.

No one spoke during the drive from the hospital to the island, and as they traveled the darkened streets of Carolina Cove, Devon's mind drifted between the past and present.

She'd had a good childhood. A stable one made richer by the people in her life. But now she wondered how much of it was a lie.

How long had her father been seeing the woman? Was she the first? The *only* affair? Were there more? If so, how many? How long had he snuck around and betrayed their mother?

There were three news vans parked in front of

the house when they arrived, but Oz drove up the driveway and across the lawn, right up to the steps so that the vehicle mostly hid their entrance.

Devon and Dara walked on either side of their mother, lending what support they could to her trembling form, while Oz hurried ahead to get the door open. Michael and Logan parked in the driveway and made sure the reporters kept their distance before the brothers jogged toward the house and joined them in the foyer.

"Come on, Mama," Devon said. "Let's get you upstairs and into something more comfortable."

"I'll be up in a minute," Logan said. "I have something to help calm her."

Devon nodded, worried about her mother's blank expression. She'd cried at first, completely heartbroken. But then she'd gone silent. Silent and unresponsive.

Devon wrapped her arm around her mom's shoulders and urged her up the first step. Her mother still wore her work clothes, and had she not cried off her makeup, she'd still look as put together as ever. The elegant, well-to-do wife of a prominent man.

It took four times as long to reach the top of the staircase as normal, but finally they made it, and

Devon steered her mother down the hall toward the master suite.

The suite consisted of two adjoining bedrooms, each with a private bath. And now that she was older and wiser—and her eyes had been opened to her father's behavior—the separate beds made the questions about her father bombard her all over again.

Her mother and father had taken on separate rooms when she and Dara were... around twelve? Fifteen? Her mother had explained that her father's ridiculously loud snoring kept her awake, but was that actually why they'd started sleeping separately? Had something happened back then? Was that why her mother had made it a summer project to redo the rooms into a two-bedroom master?

Devon felt more than a little numb herself as she walked her mother into the bathroom and urged her to go while she hunted for a nightgown. Thankfully her mother was a creature of habit, and they were in the same drawer as they'd been when Devon lived at home.

Her mother had finished and sat just staring into space. Devon paused in the doorway, gut clenched at the sight of such brokenness. "Come on, Mama. Let's get you changed."

Devon had never had the experience of caring

for her mother the way her mother had cared for her. But as she removed her mother's blouse and pulled the nightgown over her head, she remembered when her mother had dressed her as a child, lifting her arms and waiting while she slid the nightgown into place over her little-girl form.

The memory was another gut-wrenching stab to her heart, and Devon watched as her hands shook nearly as badly as her mother's.

That done, Devon found a cloth and gently washed the smeared makeup from Rayna Jo's face before tossing it toward the sink. Brushing teeth would've been next, but surely missing one night wouldn't hurt. "Bedtime, Mama," she said, leading her mother back into the bedroom.

Devon had just pulled the sheet and lightweight blanket up over her mom when a soft knock sounded on the door.

Her mother didn't move. Didn't even blink.

"It's me," Logan said from the other side.

"Come in," Devon called.

The door opened and her cousin poked his head into the room, his gaze shifting from Devon to Rayna Jo.

"You're looking more comfortable, Aunt Ray-Ray," he said softly, moving into the room. "I brought you water and something to help you sleep."

Devon watched but her mother didn't respond. "She hasn't said a word since the hospital. Is that normal?"

"She's in shock," Logan said, seating himself by Rayna Jo's side.

Logan checked her pulse and studied her for a bit before handing her the glass and urging her to take the meds. Her mother swallowed the tiny pills as ordered, and Logan smoothed her hair back from her face.

"You get some rest, Ray-Ray. I'll check on you in the morning, okay?"

Her mother shifted in the bed and curled on her side away from them, eyes dry, unseeing.

Logan tilted his head toward the door and Devon followed.

"Those should help her sleep through the night. I'll leave these here with you," he said, handing her a small bottle with a dozen or so pills inside. "Put them somewhere out of sight just in case."

"Just in case?" Devon blinked, and catching on to what he meant by the wording, she sucked in a harsh breath. "Oh."

"She'll be fine, Dev. It's just a precaution. People

process things in very different ways, and she needs time to work through this. Call me if you need me."

"Of course. Thank you."

Logan bent and gave her a quick hug and then headed out of the bedroom.

Devon retraced her steps to the bed far enough to glimpse her mother's face and saw that her eyes were closed, though tears slipped from beneath her lashes. She didn't make a sound, wasn't sobbing. Just silent tears. And that, more than anything, told Devon the depth of her mother's despair.

Devon moved to the sitting area and sat down, waiting until she heard her mother's breathing soften and even out. When she was sure Rayna Jo slept, Devon turned on a nightlight and left the bedroom to slowly make her way down the stairs.

Her feet felt heavy, her body weighted as she dragged it along when, in reality, she wanted to crumple on the steps and have a good cry herself.

But she didn't. Couldn't.

Not when the anger over her father's actions and behavior flooded her veins and she had to stay strong, at least until her mother was okay.

Devon entered the kitchen, where Dara and the others stood quietly talking. They all looked at her when she walked in, and Devon waited for someone to speak.

"She's asleep?" Logan asked.

Devon nodded.

"Wine?" Dara asked, holding up the bottle.

"Make it a double," Devon said dryly. She crossed to the island and pulled out a stool to seat herself. She glanced around the large kitchen but didn't see Michael or Oz.

"He's gone," Dara stated knowingly, her gaze direct.

Like it or not, Devon felt herself relax a bit.

"So," Logan said, downing the last of the scotch in his glass. "Do we talk about what happened or avoid it for the awkwardness that it is?"

CHAPTER FOUR

The following morning, Rayna Jo watched as the shadows of the sunrise shifted across the ceiling of the elegantly decorated room.

She'd worked hard to make their home beautiful and comfortable, and with the sun shining through the sheers, she knew she had achieved her goal.

She loved sleeping with the doors open on cool nights, listening to the sound of the waves and the rustle of the fabric as it slid against itself, billowing in the breeze.

She rolled onto her back with a frown as she tried to piece together the events that left her feeling muddled. She didn't remember changing into the nightgown she now wore. Didn't remember going to bed at all, actually.

She turned toward the door leading into the adjoining bedroom. "Richard? Are you awake?"

She pushed herself upright, and the room spun so much she sat on the edge of the bed until she was steady enough to cross the floor to the double doors.

The bedroom was empty, the bed she'd made the morning after he'd left on his business trip untouched.

But... he'd come home. Hadn't he? Or had his return been a dream?

Oh, why did her head feel so foggy?

She walked to the balcony doors overlooking the boardwalk, hoping some fresh air and sunshine would clear the cobwebs.

She flung the doors wide, lifting a hand to cover her eyes because of the brightness as she stepped outside.

She always worried when Richard traveled. She couldn't help it. The world wasn't nearly as safe as it used to be, and at sixty-five, he wasn't a young, strong man anymore.

Birds squawked and there was a pelican sitting on the edge of the balcony railing. She stared at the bird, who stared back at her. It blinked but didn't move or fly away, which she found a bit odd.

Maybe she was still dreaming?

Rayna Jo took a step toward the bird, hand outstretched, and watched as the pelican took flight. She then stared at her hand because it didn't quite seem to be attached. It... floated and blurred a bit when she moved, like she wasn't entirely in her body but outside of it.

"Mama? Mama, what are you doing? Come inside," Devon said.

Footsteps hurried across the floor, and Devon wrapped a throw around her and forcibly turned her toward the open door. "Devon, it's too hot for that."

"Mama, you're in a nightgown in front of the reporters," Devon said. "Come back inside."

Reporters? She looked over the balcony and saw people below staring up at them, hands up as they pointed cameras in their direction.

Her daughter pushed her into the bedroom and shut the doors behind them.

"Mama, why did you go out there? You knew we'd be surrounded, just like last night."

"Last night?"

"When we left the hospital."

"Did you get hurt?" She searched Devon for signs of an injury but didn't find any. "Are you all right?"

Devon drew back and gave Rayna Jo an odd look, but then her daughter tightened her hold and steered Rayna Jo to the sitting area.

"I'm okay, Mama."

"That's good. The network wouldn't want you banged and bruised on camera."

"Um. Yeah. Mama, sit down. I'll have someone get us some tea."

"Someone? Who's here?" Rayna Jo asked.

Tears brightened Devon's eyes and she blinked rapidly. Rayna Jo's heart pinched at the sight, and she stretched out her hands. The moment Devon's palms slid into hers, she *tsked*. "Honey, what's wrong? Did you and Oscar have another fight? Is he still angry with you because you took the internship in New York? You've been crying. I can tell."

"I-I'm... tired, Mama. That's all."

"I think it's more than that," Rayna Jo chided softly. "Just know that boy loves you, Devon. Even if you have to postpone the wedding for a bit, it'll all work out."

"Mama, I... Let me get the tea and we'll talk.

Okay? Don't move. Don't go outside. You stay right here and relax."

"I am tired," she said, leaning back in the chair. "I never do sleep well when your father's away on business. I can't wait for him to come home. I feel so safe when he's here in the house with me."

***

DEVON LEFT her mother in the second-floor bedroom and raced down the stairs, wishing she'd carried her cell with her so that she could've just texted Dara instead of having to go find her.

Dara sat in the living room, staring at her laptop screen, and as Devon walked into the room, she spotted Tessa and Mary Elizabeth coming up the walk toward the front door, casserole dishes in hand.

"Call Logan," Devon said. "Something's wrong with Mama."

"What's going on?" Dara asked, her frown deepening as she looked up from the computer where she worked.

"She's acting strange, talking weird. She thinks Dad is away on business, and Oz and I are still together."

"Come again?"

"Call Logan," Devon repeated, "and tell him to get over here. Zoey, too, if she's able," she said, referring to Tessa's daughter who was a psychiatrist. "I'll let the Babes in. Oh, and I told Mama we'd bring her tea."

"On it," Dara said, setting the laptop aside and pulling out her cell while she stood to head toward the kitchen.

Devon hurried to the front door to unlock it since no one had been in or out yet today. Well, other than her mother's trip to the balcony.

She swung the door wide just as the Babes made it to the top of the porch steps. "Hi."

"How is she doing?" Mary Elizabeth asked without pause.

Devon invited them in, and the Babes seemed to understand how overwhelmed she felt. They rushed inside and hugged Devon tight, and once again, she fought off tears, explaining the morning so far.

"Oh, my," Mary Elizabeth said. "Do you think she's had a stroke from the stress? Some sort of nervous breakdown?"

Devon shook her head. "I don't know. Logan said she was in shock last night. I asked Dara to text Zoey."

"Zoey is away at a conference," Tessa said. "She

should be back in time for the funeral, but she always says it's best if the person has no previous relationship to the therapist. Because they're more likely to open up."

"Logan's on the way," Dara said, joining them. "Tea's almost ready. Zoey sends her best but—"

"Yeah, a conference," Devon said.

"Give me those—and thank you," Dara added, taking the casseroles. "I'll put them away while you guys go on up."

Devon led the way with two of the Babes following, every creak of the floorboards as familiar as breathing because she'd lived most of her life in this house. Her mother and father had moved them in with Grandma when she couldn't take care of herself any longer, and Devon didn't remember a time when at least a few of the cousins or their island friends weren't bursting in and out of the front door.

Devon paused outside the bedroom and took a breath before going inside. Her mother had stayed put and seemed to be dozing. Maybe it was a side effect of the medication Logan had given her? "Mama?" she asked softly.

Rayna Jo opened her eyes and smiled before she turned her head, then lifted it from the back of the chair.

"Oh! I didn't hear the doorbell. Did we make plans, girls? I'm afraid I'm not feeling up to it today. You'll have to go without me."

Devon watched as Tessa and Mary Elizabeth exchanged a glance before moving toward their friend.

"No, no. We thought since your girls were in town, we'd come visit," Mary Elizabeth said. "Cheryl and Adaline will be here soon."

"Oh. Well, I should get dressed," Rayna Jo said.

"No rush, Mama," Devon told her. "Dara's bringing tea."

"And it's just us," Mary Elizabeth said. "You can dress after your tea or go back to bed, whatever you feel like."

Rayna Jo nodded in agreement and asked what the temperature would be for the day. "It's so bright and sunny. I think Addy and I should play hooky. Let our assistant manager handle things. It's too beautiful to spend the day inside. Maybe we could lounge on the beach for a bit? What do you say, girls?"

A sound drew Devon's attention to the door, and she turned to find Dara carrying a tea tray, followed by Cheryl and Aunt Adaline.

"I brought cups for everyone," Dara said, her smile looking forced. "How are we doing?"

A LITTLE LATER, Devon was in the kitchen washing the teacups when a soft knock sounded on the back door.

She dried her hands and peeked out the curtain to see Logan and his brother, Michael, as well as Oz. "Do they run in packs?" she muttered softly.

Devon opened the door and stepped back so that all three broad-shouldered men could enter. Like her and Dara, Logan and Michael were identical twins, though Michael's hair appeared to be a darker shade of brown than his brother's due to how short Logan wore his and the gray starting to show. Both had deep blue eyes.

"Is she doing any better?" Logan asked.

Devon shook her head, still not meeting Oz's gaze though she could feel the intensity of his stare. "It's like she doesn't remember anything. Dad's just away on business like always and... um, she thinks Oz and I are still together."

Logan frowned darkly at the news, and she knew her cousin wouldn't rest until he got help for her mom. And since she couldn't bring herself to look at Oz, she shrugged. "The Babes are with her now. Dara's on the phone with the funeral home trying to get started on the arrangements since Mom's not..." Her words trailed to a halt and she couldn't continue because she wasn't sure how. In less than twenty-four hours, things had changed so much.

Her mother had always been emotional. Of all the Babes, her mom and Mary Elizabeth seemed more like sisters due to the fact both were softer-hearted and their feelings easily hurt. They cried at commercials, when happy or sad, but this?

"Too bad Zoey's out of town," Logan said.

"I know," she whispered.

"I'll go check on her," Logan said, heading toward the staircase. "In the meantime, you might want to check out the newspaper."

Her stomach clenched into a hard knot. "Newspaper?"

Expression grim, Michael held out the paper in question, and Devon reluctantly took it. Front page was a huge article about the accident, and one of the photos from the hospital last night.

Taken when Oz had held her.

"Mom's upstairs, too?" Michael asked.

Devon nodded, distracted and horrified, barely

hearing Michael excuse himself.

That left her alone with Oz and the photo she hoped Ted wouldn't see because of the questions it would bring up.

"How are you holding up?"

A laugh burst out of her chest, the sound high-pitched as she crumpled the paper up and shoved it into the recycling bin.

"That's a good-sized group of reporters out front."

"More and more keep coming. I think they're wanting us to make a statement but... I'm not sure what to say. It's another thing on the to-do list that got pushed down when Mama woke up and... wasn't herself."

"She just needs time. It's a shock, all of it," Oz said. "Maybe you should have Adam prepare something though."

Adam was Mary Elizabeth's husband and an attorney. As far as ideas went, that wasn't a bad one. "I'll contact him."

"Dev?"

Oz's hand touched her shoulder and she shrugged it away. "I, um, should go upstairs. Be there to hear what Logan has to say."

"It'll take him a bit to assess her," Oz said. "You'll

know as soon as he knows."

She knew he was right but it didn't take the worry away. Or her extreme awareness of Oz's handsome features watching her with such tenderness. The last ten years had been kind to him. Given him a more masculine edge. "I, um, forgot to congratulate you last night. I heard you hit *New York Times.* That's fantastic."

"The Babes need to be on my publicist's advertising team. But thanks. Not bad for a neighborhood kid, huh?" he asked, fingers tucked into the pockets of his shorts.

"You always impressed with your writing."

"So did you."

She had. Once. But it had been so long since she'd written anything, she wasn't sure she could. Oz had focused all his attention on developing his skills on the writing side of journalism, whereas she'd found it more fun to be in front of the camera. But in the end, it meant chasing dreams that had separated them and ended their relationship. "Look, I... owe you an apology, Oz. A lot of them, actually. I handled things all wrong from start to finish ten years ago and—"

"Water and bridge, like I said last night."

Finally, she forced her gaze to his and found

herself sucked in by his blue eyes. Where Logan and Michael's gazes were dark blue, Oz's blazed as though there was a fire behind them, giving them even more intensity in their light blue color. His gaze had always been her downfall. One glance and she melted.

And now that Oz was a bit older, scruffier, with hints of gray on his chin and at his temples, it added to his appeal and made him even more attractive. "Is it though?"

Oz ran a hand over his hair, tousling the longer strands on top. Her fingers itched with the desire to smooth and fix, and she shoved her hands into the side pockets of her simple summer dress.

"You chose, Devon."

"I did. But that doesn't tell me whether or not you really forgive me," she said. "Or are you just pretending to because our families and histories are so... intertwined?"

A slow, sexy smile formed on his lips, and she looked away, feeling very much like the awkward schoolgirl she'd found herself becoming around him when she'd noticed him as more than a boy and her older cousin's best friend.

"You needed to do your own thing. I didn't like it. I hated it, in fact," he said. "But I'd never want you to be unhappy, Devon. Not then and especially not now."

The sweetness of his statement touched a place in the deepest recesses of her soul.

Oz was that guy. The one she'd given up and yet would never forget. Their goals and timing just hadn't been right. But everything else? That had been overwhelmingly perfect. "I-I want the same for you. To be happy, I mean."

"Then we agree," he said with that southern drawl and charm of his. "So stop worrying."

Silence followed his words, and she turned away, remembering how it had felt to be held by him even though she knew the danger of the temptation. "I was thinking of making lemonade. Would you like some? Or iced tea?"

"A New Yorker drinking sweet tea?"

A smile curled her lips. "Every girl has a vice."

A chuckle rumbled out of his chest, and she felt herself blushing at the memory the sound brought about. That of him and her and an isolated stretch of beach on one of the uninhabited islands along the Intercoastal Waterway.

"So," Oz said, stepping close to the island to peel back the lid of one of the containers the Babes had carried in. "When's your fiancé arriving?"

OZ HADN'T MEANT to bring up the subject of Devon's fiancé, but seeing as how she'd worn a ring last night... His curiosity got the best of him.

"He's... not. I mean, I haven't called him. Not yet. It was too late last night and this morning when Mama... I just haven't had a chance."

"You mean he doesn't know your father passed?" Shouldn't he have been the first person she'd called? Texted? Something?

"I-I'm not sure. He might. I mean, with as many reporters around as there are, and Oliver Beck's involvement... He might."

"But if that's the case, it means he hasn't contacted you, either," Oz pointed out.

Devon moved away from him and went to the fridge, opening the door and staring inside like she searched for answers among the produce and milk.

"I told you, it's... complicated. He's very busy, so I thought I'd wait until the final arrangements were made so that I could relay them."

"He should be here for you. The next few days—"

She slammed the fridge door shut and glared at

him. "Stop. Okay? You do not get to judge a relationship you know nothing about."

"And neither does your family, so it seems."

"I asked you not to mention anything because it's
very new and... We got engaged yesterday, okay?
Before Dara called about Dad. Literally, *seconds*
before."

He whistled softly. "That is new. But given the
seriousness of the situation, why didn't Ted come
with you?" He watched as her hands fisted.

"Because he can't get away that quickly. And...
he's running for office and he needs to steer clear of
scandal—which I understand given the circumstances. I'd avoid this, too, if I could."

The man was a coward. Couldn't she see that?
No decent human being would allow someone they
loved to go through what Devon faced alone. "He
should be here with you. No excuses."

Devon yanked open the fridge door again and
pulled out a bowl of grapes only to open the freezer
next and shove them inside.

Frozen grapes?

"It's easy to judge something you don't
understand."

"I do understand. Your father was in a horrible

car accident, in critical condition. The circumstances are unpleasant—"

"*Unpleasant?*"

"I'm being kind," he stated without pause. "The point is any man worth marrying should be here by your side. Period."

"Again, you know nothing of it. Now *kindly* leave the topic alone and stay out of my love life."

"Doesn't sound as though there is one," he murmured before he could stop himself.

Devon released a small shriek of frustration that left him wincing, and he watched as she stomped from the room into the breakfast area and out of sight.

"Still working your magic, I see," Logan said softly from behind him.

Oz turned to find his best friend's twin watching him with an amused expression. "I've got the touch."

"Do I want to know what that was about?" Logan asked.

"Probably. But it'll mean asking her, and I recommend you proceed with caution if you do. How's Rayna Jo?"

"Logan?" Devon called from the other room, apparently identifying his voice.

Seconds later she'd made her way back to the

kitchen, and Oz watched as she made a beeline for her cousin.

"How is she?" Devon asked.

"Physically, she's fine," Logan said. "Emotionally... that's another story."

"What can we do?" Devon asked. "What's happening?"

"After examining Rayna Jo I called Zoey. We believe it's something called dissociative amnesia. It's a disorder that's caused by high stress or trauma. Rayna Jo's also experiencing conversion disorder and feels like she's not quite in her body. Thankfully neither is typically permanent, and they usually resolve on their own. But they can last several days... or weeks."

"*Weeks?*" Devon asked.

"I can order an MRI to check for a stroke but... I just don't think that's it. She has no speech impediment, no paralysis or slurring. Based on what's going on, I think Zoey's right and it's emotional, especially given Rayna Jo's history of anxiety and depression. For now, our best advice is for her to rest and stay calm. It'll give her mind time to adjust to what it already knows."

"That's it? There's *nothing* we can do?" Devon asked.

Oz watched as his friend shook his head and, in the process, seemingly broke Devon's heart.

"Keep her away from the television and radio. Protect her from the mess outside. She thinks the reporters are here because you've landed such a big position in New York."

"But that was ten years ago."

"Yeah, but think about it. After you got the offer, you had a couple local news crews around."

"Slow news week," she muttered.

"Rayna Jo's mind has fallen back on that memory. It's a safe answer to what her mind isn't able to process right now."

Oz stared at Devon, gut tight at the frustrating news. "She'll be okay, Dev."

"She's *not* okay," she said, sliding him a glare. "None of this is okay. How can we have a funeral o-or *any*thing when she doesn't even remember that Dad's—"

Devon's voice broke, the word choked, and Oz stepped forward to pull her stiff body into his arms to hold. She leaned on him for a moment, just a moment, head down, nose buried against his chest, before she inhaled and shoved him away. He reluctantly released her and watched as she crossed her arms across her chest and walked several steps away from them to the kitchen sink to gather her emotions.

"Devon, I'm not sure what to tell you about the arrangements for Uncle Richard," Logan said. "But due to the accident and police-ordered autopsy, it will take several days for his body to be released. That buys some time. Hopefully she'll come around by then."

"And if she hasn't?" she asked softly.

"We'll have to play it by ear. I took some blood samples and am heading to the hospital to get them processed, just to rule out something I might've missed. I'll let you know as soon as I know something."

Logan paused on his way to the kitchen door and brushed a kiss over Devon's head. "Love you, kid. Hang in there."

Logan murmured goodbye and left quietly, and silence descended on the room.

Oz watched as Devon slowly turned to face him. His chest squeezed at the sight of her, and all he wanted to do was grab her up and take her away from the pain. Go back to the days when a music-blasted ride to the south end of the island could cure most things. At least for a while. "What do you need me to do? Name it."

"I don't know," she whispered, the words sounding raw.

A long silence followed the statement but he waited patiently.

"Um... you're a writer," she said finally. "Have you ever written a eulogy about a cheating husband and father?"

CHAPTER FIVE

Maybe it was wrong to pawn the responsibility of her father's eulogy off on Oz, but considering her own emotional state due to the circumstances, Devon felt she was far too focused on her father's last moments with another woman to write of favorite childhood memories, accolades, and love.

She couldn't praise the man's good deeds when she drowned in the depths of his betrayal, especially in light of her mother's inability to cope.

Regardless, Oz agreed to do the chore, and she left him in her father's study while she went to her bedroom and pulled out her phone to call Ted.

She needed to hear Ted's voice. Needed to talk to him. Especially after the hugs she'd received from

Oz had made her angrier that Ted wasn't there to offer comfort as she'd asked him to be.

And all the feelings and emotions dredged up by Oz's touch? *Proximity*. That was all.

"Hello? Dev, is that you?"

"Yeah. Hi," she said simply.

"Sorry, babe. I've been meaning to call all morning but things got hectic."

"They've been a little hectic here, too," she said, unable to keep her voice as even as she'd have liked. "Dad passed last night."

"Yeah, I heard."

So he had heard—but he couldn't take two seconds out of his day to call? "When are you coming down? You'll have a few days to make plans. They have to do an autopsy first and then release the body to the funeral home."

"Devon, have you seen the papers?"

"Papers?"

"Who's the guy?"

"What guy?"

"The guy holding you in the pictures?"

Her mind flashed to the scene at the hospital when the reporters had burst into the waiting area. "Oh. Ted, that wasn't what it looked like. They literally captured the moment we learned that Dad passed. Oz was... just being a friend."

"Your ex-fiancé, Oz?"

She grimaced. "He's a longtime family *friend*," she said to Ted. "It wasn't like that. I promise. He was just... He gave me a hug. Had you been there, it would've been you," she said, hoping the statement would hit home. "Ted... I don't want to fight. I want you here, with me. Please?"

"We talked about this. You know I can't."

Can't? "My father *died*. Are you seriously saying you can't come to the funeral because of how it might reflect on you?"

"Justin is working twenty hours a day doing damage control," Ted said, referring to his campaign manager. "And that picture of you with your ex certainly didn't help. He's heard the comment *like father, like daughter* more than once."

Were people really so petty? "So let's show the world it was nothing by giving them a united front with you at my side as I *bury* my father."

"Babe, you know I can't drop everything and leave. I have meetings and events I can't miss."

"That's why I stressed the fact that you have a few days to prepare and rearrange your schedule," she said softly.

"I'm sorry about your loss, but the best thing for you to do is steer clear of Oz and come home," he said. "We'll show a united front here, okay? Yeah, yeah, I'm coming," he said to someone. "Devon, I gotta run. Flowers are on the way. I'll try to call you tonight."

The phone clicked in her ear without so much as a goodbye or *love you* from her fiancé. She thought of the ring in her upstairs dresser, now hidden from anyone who might wander by and see it lying about.

Reality set in with the weight of an anchor dragging the bottom of the ocean. She didn't like it. She didn't like it at all.

She redialed the number but of course Ted didn't answer. "You didn't call me even though you knew my father had passed, and now you're too busy to be with me when I need you the most. More than I've ever needed your support. That says a lot, Ted. Too much, in fact. If protecting your image is more important than being here for me for my father's funeral then... this will never work. We will never work. I'll return the ring when I get back to New York."

Men hated being challenged in that way but she couldn't help it. There was no legitimate excuse for him not to attend the funeral. No excuse at all!

She lowered the phone and pressed the button to end the call, tempted to throw the darn thing.

A noise sounded behind her, and she whirled around to find Dara, Michael, and Oz all standing there, all watching her.

"We, uh, came to see if you wanted to go to the funeral home and meet with the director," Dara said. "The Babes are going to stay with Mama."

Devon swallowed the lump in her throat and shoved the phone into the pocket of her dress. "Let me get my purse."

She felt Oz's gaze on her as she stalked by them and wondered if he'd overheard the comment she'd made about him being a friend. That it should've been Ted holding her. It had probably hurt Oz, but it couldn't be helped, she thought as she left the room.

"Did I hear that right?" Devon heard Michael ask after she'd stepped out. "Dev is engaged even though we've never met the guy?"

"I'm not," she informed them softly. "Not anymore."

THIRTY MINUTES LATER, Devon stared at the coffins on display and wondered if *she* wasn't having a conversion disorder symptom.

Because this?

This didn't feel real. Not on any level.

Losing a parent was inevitable, but she'd hoped she wouldn't face this day for a very, very long time.

And under the circumstances?

She'd purposely kept herself away from the news and social media, but she knew she couldn't hide forever.

"You know, you haven't said much about all of this," Dara said softly.

"I don't care which coffin. It's going into the ground so what does it matter?"

"I meant about Dad, the accident... the woman. Even last night when we were in the kitchen talking, you didn't say anything. Not a word, even though I know you're boiling inside. I can tell."

She'd almost forgotten how she and Dara shared that twin thing. Sometimes it felt like they shared the same brain waves or something. "It's best I don't comment. Nothing I have to say would be kind at the moment."

Dara released a whoosh of air that resembled a grunt.

"You've definitely got more willpower than me, then. 'Cause I'm *pissed*. I mean, come on. She was twenty-freaking-*three*. Was his ego really that big that he thought a woman—any woman—that young would be interested in anything other than his money? How could he do this to Mom? To us? That girl was twelve years younger than we are. It's just *sick*."

Devon closed her eyes and squeezed them tight to ease the burning. "This isn't the place, Dara."

"No one's around. The guys are down the hall with the director."

"But there are probably cameras on us, maybe microphones."

"Like I care at this point. It's not like people don't know. It's all over the radio, the papers, the internet. Have you seen all of the memes?"

Memes? Okay, so no wonder Justin was doing damage control.

"It's a good thing Mom checked out. I wouldn't mind it at the moment if it meant escaping this train wreck."

Devon wandered over to a black casket with only a few silver accents. "This one. It's... subtle."

"Like that's going to help," Dara muttered. "I

wonder if they have red. You know, like a scarlet letter? Let him be what he is."

Devon turned and faced her younger-by-eight-minutes sister. "Dara, I get it. I'm angry, too, but our anger is only going to hurt us. Not Dad and not... *her*."

"I know but how can you be so calm? It's annoying."

"I'm not calm. I'm"—*anything but*—"resigned. Dad screwed up but Mom needs us to help her. To get her through this because she obviously can't cope with it on her own."

"Yeah, well, like I said, a fugue state would be welcome right now." Dara ran her hand over the braid hanging over her shoulder. "Screw it. Let's get that one," she said, indicating the one Devon had chosen. "So we can call this done and get out of here."

Decision made, they turned to go back toward the office when the director appeared, Michael and Oz in the office doorway behind him, reenforcing Devon's belief that there were cameras in the room.

The next step was choosing flowers, music, those who would speak. Finally the chore was finished, and as soon as the body was released, they could go about the business of burying their father.

They walked out of the funeral home and into the heat of the day, waiting beneath the covered awning while the guys walked to the car and brought it up to the entrance.

"The air's a lot different than the streets of New York, huh?" Dara stated.

She hadn't realized the breath she'd inhaled was so loud. "I'd forgotten how fresh salt air is."

"You've stayed away too long."

"See one, see us both," Devon said, quoting their mantra from their teen years when attendance was required at different events and one didn't want to go.

"It's good to be back, though, isn't it?" Dara asked. "Even though it's for this?"

The last ten years had consisted of exactly two short trips home to Carolina Cove. Both times she'd managed to avoid Oz, though she told herself she would've been fine had she seen him.

It was a lie though. She'd glimpsed Oz's expression after she'd left the message on Ted's machine, and despite Oz's attempts to hide his thoughts, he'd failed.

Her telling Ted she'd give the ring back had apparently brought *their* past to mind, and Oz wasn't as over it as he said he was.

And she felt bad for that. He was a good guy. Did he date? There were plenty of women who'd accept an invitation if he asked.

"I'm saying," Dara continued, "it's home."

It was. And she'd missed it. But sometimes you couldn't go home again. Like the saying *not all who wander are lost...* She'd found her way, taken her own path.

"There they are. Are you hungry?" Dara asked. "You've lost weight since I saw you last."

"The cameras add it on, trust me." And with all the gorgeous up-and-coming wannabes, she needed to keep in top shape.

"Yeah, well, you need at least one solid meal before we head back to the house. Maybe your old favorite of a Tanglewood burger and beer-battered onion rings?"

RAYNA JO TRIED and failed to fight her fatigue. She didn't remember ever being this tired in her life, not even when the girls were babies and on opposite sleep schedules.

While Tessa and Cheryl talked about Tessa's upcoming date with her ex-husband, Rayna Jo felt

Adaline's gaze on her. Her sister seemed a bit off, and Rayna Jo blamed it on Addy's worry. "Stop staring. I'm fine. Nothing a nap won't fix," she said.

Tessa and Cheryl stopped talking and now Rayna Jo held all of their attention. "Girls, what is wrong with all of you? I've been under the weather before. You need to go home and stop worrying about me."

"We're just visiting," Mary Elizabeth said. "We'll leave you be once the twins get back."

Rayna Jo pushed herself up from the settee and hated the head rush that resulted. The room spun like a kaleidoscope, but when it settled, she moved toward the bathroom. Along the way, she paused at the window. "They're still down there," she murmured, seeing the television vans below. "I know Devon's big-city job offer is amazing for a small town, but I wouldn't think it would be *that* newsworthy. Aren't there other more important stories to be covered?"

"It's a mystery," Mary Elizabeth said as she moved to where Rayna Jo stood. "Let's get away from the window."

Urged toward the bathroom, Rayna Jo continued on, closing the door behind her. She paused again when she spied herself in the mirror. When had she gotten so old? The wrinkles and lines and bags beneath her eyes, the gray she needed to have colored. She should see if Tessa could squeeze her in before Richard returned. She wanted to look her best for him.

Minutes later she left the bathroom and frowned when the conversation among the Babes stopped. "What's going on? What are you whispering about?"

"We're just saying you should try to rest," Cheryl said.

"Actually, I was hoping Tessa might color my hair. Richard will be home soon, and I don't want to have to go one evening when we could be together. He travels so often these days."

"What a great idea," Tessa said quickly. "I'll run down to the shop and get what I need."

"I can come with you. You must have other appointments today?"

"No, no. I took the day off and you'll be more comfortable if I do it here," Tessa said. "It's no problem."

Tessa got up and headed toward the door, and Rayna Jo returned to the settee. "So what's really going on? You're acting strange. What's with all of you?"

THAT EVENING OZ sat in Richard Teeks's study, trying to write the eulogy Devon had requested. He'd hoped the setting would inspire him, but instead he kept getting distracted by the memories the house held.

Memories of Richard were few and far between. The man had been there in the peripheral, but now, in light of what had happened, Oz suspected it wasn't the first time the man had strayed.

He forced his mind away from the personal side of Rayna Jo's marriage and focused on the task at hand.

As a professional author, it should've been easy. He wrote thriller fiction. He made up complicated stories that had plenty of twists and turns and surprises to keep his readers reading until the very last page.

But whenever he put pen to paper, the words just weren't there for Richard. How could he put a positive spin on something that hurt the people he loved? Devastated Rayna Jo to the point she couldn't cope?

He tossed the pen down and leaned back in the tufted leather chair. Richard Teeks had always struck him as being a little too... smooth. Always "on."

The girls were smart. And Dara... he'd be surprised if she wasn't using her cyber expertise to track down every bit of information she could regarding her father's other life.

The door to the study opened, and he looked up to see Rayna Jo walk in. Her smile fell when she saw him, but she quickly forced it back into place.

"I'm sorry. I saw the light and thought Richard had finally made it home."

Oz sat forward in the chair, deftly sliding a sheet of blank paper over his failed attempts. "Uh, no. Just me. Dara and Devon said I could use the office."

"Of course. Are you writing? Tell me about your latest book. I just know you're going to sell to New York soon. I've read your articles in the newspaper and they're quite good."

He hadn't written for the paper in five years, not since quitting his day job to write full-time. "Thank you. I appreciate that."

"May I read it?"

"Uh, no. Don't take offense but I'm particular. I don't like to show my work before it's ready."

"Of course. I understand." Rayna Jo tilted her head to the side, her gaze narrowing on him. "Oscar,

I know you're worried about Devon moving to New York but there's no need. She's excited about the job offer, but there's no guarantee the internship will turn into anything permanent. She'll be back before you know it. Just let her enjoy her moment in the spotlight knowing we've bought the dress and the church is booked. It'll all work out fine. You'll see."

Her words gutted him and brought back a similar conversation she'd had with him when the Babes had thrown an engagement party for them, held the day *after* Devon had received the job offer for the network she still worked for today.

Devon had pitched herself as part of a major online marketing recruitment without telling him because, according to her, she hadn't expected to win.

But she had won. And they'd started fighting as soon as she'd told him and kept fighting right up until she asked him to move to New York City and leave his home and life behind.

The following day at the party, Rayna Jo had found him alone, struggling to control his frustration after yet another round with Devon.

"Oh, dear. Did I say something wrong?" Rayna Jo asked.

Snapped back to the present by the question, Oz

managed a smile and stood. "Not at all. It'll work out if it's meant to, right?"

"Exactly," she said in her soothing voice, relief smoothing her features that she hadn't said too much. "My mother used to say some people are just sea glass and sand."

"How so?" he asked, curious.

"Well," she said, coming deeper into the room, "it takes the pain of breaking and the grit of the sand rubbing the raw edges to make sea glass smooth and beautiful. People search for it every day, but they consider it trash unless it's polished down and pretty."

"So am I the glass or the sand?" he asked.

She tilted her head to one side, her expression softening to motherly love. "I hate to say it, Oscar, but you're the glass, dear. Red glass."

"Why red?" he asked, fascinated by the way her mind worked and the bits of story that were beginning to appear in his head.

"Every color has meaning. Green is envy. White purity. Blue contentment. But red is rare and especially hard to find. It means love. Oh, Oscar, I *know* how much you love Devon. I see it every time you look at her, but my daughter... she has sand in her veins. Give her this opportunity. Let her get it out of her system and then she'll be ready to settle down."

He inhaled and tried to get a grip on the emotions her words had brought about. "In New York," he stated.

"No, no. We won't let that happen. We'll convince her to come home. You'll see."

But that hadn't happened. And he hated that it would be yet another aspect Rayna Jo would have to remember. That only one of her daughters lived in town, though Dara traveled quite a bit for work and was rarely home. "I, um, should get back to work. And you should be resting, Rayna Jo. Not worrying about us."

"A mother always worries, dear."

"Hey, Oz, have you seen— Mama, there you are," Devon said. "She's in the study," Devon called.

Dara's footsteps hurried down the hall, and she poked her head into the room next.

Devon and Dara looked so similar yet so different, mostly because one had in fact broken him, then left with the tide as Rayna Jo had said.

"Hey. Are we interrupting?" Dara asked.

"Never," Rayna Jo said to her girls. "Come join us."

"Actually, Mama, you should eat something. I

heated up some of Mary Elizabeth's famous home-made potato soup. Would you like some?"

Dara entered and gently ushered Rayna Jo out of the room, but Devon stood just inside the doorway, silent.

"I'm going to head out and try to get this done tonight if I can," he said, indicating the scribbled sheets.

"Thank you. For writing it."

"Of course." He narrowed his gaze on her and stepped forward. "You okay?"

"Fine."

"Want to talk about it?"

"No."

He shoved his hands into his front pockets to keep himself from reaching for her. He hated that she kept so much bottled up inside. She always had. "Have you heard from your—Ted?"

"I don't want to talk about it," she said.

"Devon, it's not healthy for you or Dara to push all of this down just because of your mom's reaction."

"I don't think it would help anyone if Dara or I lost it, too."

"Fine, but you still need to talk. If not to me or Dara, then find someone. Anyone."

She turned as though to go but paused.

"I heard what Mama said to you. About the glass. I'm sorry I hurt you. I wish I could go back and... handle it better."

"You were right to not to let anyone curtail your dreams."

"I was. But I was awful about it, too. Dara told me you... you waited at the airport for my arrival. That's where you were when I called things off. I am truly sorry, Oz."

"It wasn't the best day, I'll admit."

"I know. I just... gambled on you loving me enough to follow me to New York even though I *knew* you didn't want to leave Carolina Cove. Truthfully, I think I tried to make you move to the city by applying for that job, even though we'd already discussed where we'd live, and you made it clear you didn't want to leave."

He wasn't sure what to say except, "It wasn't a matter of not loving you enough, Devon."

"It... wasn't?"

He moved toward her, not stopping until he was able to breathe in the subtle scent of her soap or lotion and see the tiny flecks of gold in her amazing blue-green eyes.

Unable to help himself, he lifted his hand and brushed a tendril from her cheek. "No. It was that you obviously weren't ready to settle down, and I knew I had to give you the space and freedom you needed. Even if it killed me to let you go."

His gaze dropped to the pulse racing in her throat, visible and tantalizing. He took another step and allowed his hand to drift from her cheek to her neck, his thumb brushing over the spot.

His attention shifted when her lips parted to draw in more air, and he focused on the soft pink of them, lowering his head—

"Yo, Oz, you ready to head out?" Michael called from somewhere in the house.

Devon gasped and stumbled back several steps, chest rising and falling, eyes wide at what had almost happened.

"I-I should go."

"Devon?"

She held up a hand as though that would stop the awareness of what had almost been.

"I'm *engaged*, Oz."

A low huff left his chest. "I heard you on the phone, sweetheart. You're returning the ring. That means you're not."

CHAPTER SIX

I heard you on the phone, sweetheart. You're returning the ring. That means you're not.

The following morning, Devon trudged downstairs with all the energy and enthusiasm of a slug or a sloth or one of the other slow-as-molasses animals she didn't have the brain power to name at the moment.

She'd tossed and turned all night, dreams filled with the almost kiss from Oz, her phone call to Ted, and all the things currently wrong in her life.

Wasn't it enough to be burying her father under the circumstances? For her to seemingly be engaged to a man who wasn't there for her when she needed him so now she wasn't and the breakup conversation had taken place in a voicemail? Was she really going to add Oz into the mix just for giggles?

Stop it.

The kiss hadn't happened. Everything was *fine*. And Ted...

He'd sent flowers. A huge bouquet of assorted beauties and a card simply marked with *thinking of you, T.*

The sight had saddened her and made her feel... He couldn't even write his name? Sign it with love?

Was she being too picky? Had he sent the flowers before or after she'd called him back and left the message? He'd said flowers were on the way but had they been ordered at that point?

Was she being overly sensitive due to Ted's comments about protecting his image? Or maybe he was still upset about the newspaper photo of her and Oz?

A part of her understood Ted's reasons. She really did. The political scene Ted pursued was rife with scandals that often tainted a campaign and hindered an election. Even though they hadn't officially announced their engagement, they'd dated for a year, attended events together. Everyone knew they were a couple.

Oz aside, surely the American public would

understand that every household had *that* family member. While the Teekses had been blessed up until a few days ago to be free of that stigma, her father had hit a home run with his scandalous behavior. She understood why Ted was being cautious. But still...

It hurt and confused her even more.

She inhaled and sighed as she reached the bottom tread.

Coffee. She needed coffee.

Stat.

When she entered the kitchen, her mother and Dara were already there. Rayna Jo stood at the stove, making her island-famous crepes, and Devon's mouth instantly began to water at the sight. "Oh, Mama, you have *no* idea how often I crave those."

Rayna Jo smiled at Devon.

"I thought you might like them. I don't fix them nearly as much as I used to. Especially with your father traveling so much. I just make them for the Babes every now and again."

Dara met Devon's gaze at the statement and waved the jug of orange juice she held.

"Mama insists on mimosas. You up for it?"

"Can't think of any reason not to be," Devon

said. With the funeral arrangements made, there was little to do but wait and avoid the reporters outside.

As they settled into breakfast a few minutes later, the home telephone rang, and Dara checked the caller ID.

"It's the fu— Uh, I have to take this," she said, getting up from the table and excusing herself.

Devon watched her go with a knot in her stomach. If the funeral home was calling, that meant her father's body had probably been released for burial. That also meant they'd have to navigate the service with their mother. Somehow. "Mama? Have you... heard from Dad?"

"No. It's strange, too, because he always calls if he's going to be delayed."

Devon watched as her mother's expression pinched with her statement.

"But don't you worry. He'll be in touch soon. I'm sure of it," Rayna Jo said. "He won't want to miss seeing you home."

"The, um, Babes are coming over again today. Your hair looks good, by the way. Tessa did a great job yesterday."

"She always does—and thank you. You girls are so beautiful and young, it makes me feel old."

"Oh, hush up. You look at least ten years younger than your age. You have nothing to worry about."

Devon watched as her mother's gaze fastened on the crepe cooking in front of her.

"A woman always worries as she ages. I'm afraid one day your father will wake up and only see an old woman."

What a strange thing to say. Unless... "Mama, have you and Dad had words? Been fighting?"

"No, sweetheart. Merely the musings of a woman past her prime."

A knock sounded at the back door, and Devon reluctantly moved to look out the glass, spotting Logan on the other side. She hurried across the room to let him inside. "Did the test results show anything?" she asked in a low voice instead of a hello.

Logan shook his head. "They were perfect, which reinforces our diagnosis."

"What are you two whispering about over there?" Rayna Jo asked. "Logan, come have a crepe."

"Oh, man. You know those are my favorite," he said, rubbing his hands together like the excitement was too much.

He stopped by Rayna Jo and kissed her on her cheek, and Devon moved to the cabinet to get him a plate and utensils.

"Mimosas?" Logan asked, grinning. "Ray-Ray, are you celebrating?"

"It's not often that I have *both* my girls home with me. I wanted to do something special before they leave. I hate that Richard isn't home to enjoy their company, but I'm also glad to have them all to myself."

"We should try to plan a trip or something once a year, just us," Devon said. "Would you like that, Mama? Maybe take a cruise to the Bahamas? Or Alaska?"

"Maybe. I don't like being away from home. Or Richard. He's promised me that he'll retire soon," her mother said. "Maybe we could all go? Make it a family vacation like we used to take."

Devon forced a smile and shifted her attention to Logan, noting that his gaze was filled with worry before he hid it behind his doctor's smile.

"Thanks," he said when Devon handed him the plate.

They exchanged a look and then set about helping Rayna transfer the cream cheese crepes to the table along with some blueberries.

The questions she'd asked before Logan's arrival were dropped for now, but maybe her mother would think about them, and it might bring something to mind?

Logan had just dug into his food when Dara returned, and soon the kitchen was filled with laughter when they gathered around the breakfast area and started reminiscing on their childhood antics.

Devon loved watching her mother laugh to the point of tears. Until the laughter stopped but the tears kept flowing. "Mama? Are you all right?"

Her mother lifted her cloth napkin to her face and sobbed into it.

"Yes. I'm sorry. Oh, I don't know what's come over me," she said, dabbing at her eyes.

"It's okay, Mama."

"No worries," Logan said to his aunt. "You're just tired."

"I didn't sleep well last night. I had the most awful dreams," Rayna Jo said. "Maybe I sh-should go lie down again but... I need to get to work. I hate leaving Addy alone at the shop, and I didn't go yesterday."

"Dara or I can go help," Devon said. "Don't worry about that."

"Absolutely," Dara said. "We've got you covered."

"You wouldn't m-mind? I shouldn't ask, but I don't feel well and just can't seem to *st-stop*," Rayna Jo said, her choked voice squeaky high as she sobbed.

"Where are the pills I left?" Logan asked Devon.

She left the room to go fetch them, because she'd hidden them from her mother as Logan ordered, and returned to find Dara and Logan helping Rayna Jo up the stairs.

"Oh, the dishes. I left a mess."

"Mama, don't worry about that. We'll take care of it," Dara said.

Logan urged her mother on to her room and then took the bottle from Devon while Dara tucked their mother into bed.

Logan checked the paper wrapping and then opened it to pour two pills in his hand.

"Take these. Here's some water," he said, using the capped bottle from the bedside table.

Her mother managed to swallow despite the tears and turned her face into the pillow.

"I'm so s-sorry. I don't know why I'm crying."

Dara sat on one side of the bed, gently stroking Rayna Jo's shoulder, while Devon curled up on the other side, cuddling her mother close. "It's okay, Mama. Sometimes we all just need a good cry."

"But *why?* Something feels wrong. What's happening to me?"

OZ LIFTED his head when he heard an engine and gravel crunch in his driveway. Michael got out of his Jeep and lifted his chin in hello before bounding up the steps to the porch, where Oz sat facing the ocean.

"Still working on it?" his best friend asked.

The eulogy had taken hours and hours to write, with multiple attempts tossed into the trash. "I'm getting closer."

"Thanks for doing that, man. I know the cousins appreciate it, but so do I. I'm not sure I'd know what to say."

Oz nodded and set the pages aside. "You heading over there?"

"Yeah. I took the rest of the week off and stopped by to see if you wanted to go with."

Oz inhaled and shifted his gaze out to the ocean. "I do but I'm not sure I should."

"What's that mean? Did something happen between you and Dev?"

He wasn't one to kiss and tell, but talking didn't seem to be such a bad idea. "We... had a moment."

"A moment," Michael repeated. "What does that mean?"

"It means we almost kissed."

"Almost?"

Was he going to repeat everything? "Last night. We were talking and we were about to kiss when you yelled to see if I was ready to leave. Great timing, by the way."

"Ah, man. I wondered why you were such a bear on the way home. Sorry about that. I figured it was just because of Devon supposedly being engaged."

"She's not now," he corrected. "She's giving the ring back."

"Good thing. I mean, where is this guy? He should've come with her."

Oz glared at the pages in front of him and nodded his head. "I asked her that myself. Told her he should be here, supporting her."

"At least she's aware of his loser qualities now. Do you know if she's talked to him since?"

"No. No clue."

"Well, if you're done for now, why not come with me? You can test the waters again today."

He wanted to. He did. But he also reminded himself of what had happened last time. "I'm not sure that's a good idea."

Michael stared at him with the knowing look of a longtime friend. "You afraid of getting attached in case she leaves again?"

"Her life is in New York. So's the guy."

"Yeah, but after all of this with her dad, do you really think she'll still go back? Leave Rayna Jo? Her home is here," Michael said, a scowl on his face. "And now she's not engaged so…"

"Regardless, I'm going to pass," Oz said. "I might walk over later. Text me if something needs done, though, and I'll pitch in."

Michael tapped the porch railing with a hand and nodded.

"Yeah, okay. Later."

Oz lifted his head in a nod of goodbye and watched as Michael retraced his steps and backed out of the driveway.

When his friend was out of sight, Oz got up and took the pages inside, deciding a break might be the next step. He'd always found that a walk on the sand cleared his head and refilled the writing well, so to speak, and given the emotions tied to this particular document, he needed all the clarity he could get.

He wanted to get it right. No, not right. Perfect. It had to be perfect. Especially under the circumstances.

Oz locked up and jogged down the steps, crossed the street to the boardwalk, and then took the first bridge over the dunes to the shore.

His father had met a woman visiting from Florida and hit it off two years ago. They'd married a year later and now spent winters there and summers in the mountains. Oz had bought the house from his father and was grateful to have access to all of the homes whenever he wanted to visit. But Carolina Cove was and always would be home.

The sea breeze made the hot, muggy day tolerable. He paused long enough to take off his flip-flops and shove them in his back pocket for safe keeping. He'd lost several pairs over the years to people stealing them when left behind near the dunes.

Umbrellas and beach chairs crowded the sand, and the pier nearly looked to be shoulder to shoulder with fishermen lining the railings and tourists ambling down the middle and out to the T.

Summer was his least favorite time on the island, but the introverted writer in him also liked the bustle of traffic and range of accents he heard as he strolled along the water's edge.

Oz walked beneath the pier, and the sudden change from sunlight to shade left him momentarily blinded. Maybe that's why he didn't recognize Devon until she was right up on him.

"Hey," he said, shoving his sunglasses on top of his head. "Sorry, the light change got me."

She paused and bent, hands on her knees while she caught her breath from her run.

"No problem. I, um, managed to sneak out for a bit while Mama's sleeping."

"How's she doing?" he asked, watching the expressions flickering across her beautiful face.

"Not good. She kind of had a breakdown this morning. Logan was there and he gave her something to calm her down, but she couldn't stop crying, even though she didn't know why. It freaked her out."

"Understandable," he said, studying her. "How are you doing?"

Oz saw the way she stiffened at the query.

"About last night..."

"What about it?"

She yanked on the bill of the baseball cap she wore, pulling it even lower to shade her gorgeous eyes.

"That was... What I mean is you caught me off guard. But nothing's changed between us."

He crossed his arms over his chest and hated that

the cap kept him from fully seeing her face. "I dunno about that. I think a lot of things have changed."

"Not the big things, the important things," she said. "My life is in New York now."

Her words echoed his statement to Michael, but it didn't mean he hadn't recognized the bit of hope that had sprung up somewhere in his psyche. "Life is wherever you make it, Devon. And this will always be your home."

"This hasn't been home for ten years," she said, finally tilting her head back to stare up at him, stubborn expression in place. "And I'm—"

"Don't say engaged."

"Well, I am still in possession of the ring so—"

"A ring you don't wear on top of the fact he's not here when you need him, no one has met him... Want me to continue?"

"Facts are facts, Oz. Maybe it's semantics or—I don't know what it is but until I hand over the ring I feel as though I am still...entangled. I'm not going to argue about this with you. I just wanted to say that... there can't be a repeat of last night. Ever."

"Got to you that much, eh?" A huff of frustration left her and he grinned. "You can't deny it, sweetheart. I felt it, too."

"I *am* denying it."

"Oh? Let's try it then. One kiss," he said, lowering his hands and stepping toward her. "So you can prove there's nothing left of the chemistry we've always had."

"I don't have to prove anything to you. Besides... we would *never* work."

"You don't know that."

"I do know that, and if it's not enough, let me remind you that I'm en—"

He lowered his head and trapped the word between their lips, the cap she wore hitting his temple in the process.

She stood with her back to a piling, and with him in front of her, it afforded them all the privacy possible on the summer-crowded beach.

Until Devon apparently came to her senses and shoved him away.

Her lashes fluttered and he saw the effect she'd never been able to hide from him. The kiss had stirred memories, feelings, emotions from their past together.

A child's happy shriek sounded nearby, but he didn't take his gaze off of Devon. "Looks like things with us work just fine," he said softly. "Why don't we—"

"*Don't.*"

"Devon—"

She wouldn't look at him but turned without another word, tugging the cap back down over her face once more from its kiss-skewed position.

Short of chasing her down the beach, there was little he could do except let her process what had happened and go from there.

Still, he couldn't help but wonder where it could go when she was right—nothing had really changed...

Unless he could get her to see she was needed and wanted—*loved*—here more than anywhere else?

"WHAT ARE WE GOING TO DO?" Dara asked Devon that evening.

Devon blinked, drawn out of her dazed state and the memory of the kiss with Oz that had shattered her in so many ways.

She'd finished her run and come back to the house to shower and change, avoiding the television crews still parked outside by walking several streets out of the way so that she could sneak down alleys and yards to enter from the back door unnoticed.

After the shower, she'd texted Ted the details for

her father's funeral but nothing else. His attendance would tell her what she needed to know.

Especially since he still hadn't responded to her voicemail.

The Babes had stayed until dinnertime, then left to care for husbands. As the only single amongst the Babes, Tessa had stayed a bit longer, until time for her date.

Now the moon rose high over the ocean and the house was eerily quiet. "Do about what?" she asked.

"The funeral. The fact that it'll happen day after tomorrow? What's going on with you? Have you heard a word I said?" Dara asked.

Devon rubbed her gritty eyes and grimaced. "Sorry. I'm tired. I'm not used to the heat anymore. That run got me today piled on top of everything here."

"Uh-huh. Is it that... or Oz's conspicuous absence from the house today?"

Devon heard the insinuation layering Dara's tone and chose to ignore it. "What do you think we should do about the funeral? I'm open for suggestions," she said, trying to stay on topic.

"I'll let you off the hook for now, but we're returning to that subject soon. As to suggestions, as much as I hate it, maybe Mom could skip it? Once she's back to normal, we could take her and do a small gathering with just us? I'm sure one of the Babes could stay with her while we attend."

"She would never forgive herself for missing it, though," Devon said.

"Maybe. But that sentiment *was* before finding out Dad was a lying cheater."

Sometimes the truth sucked. Like now. "How long can we keep her from watching television? Or reading the news? I'm blown away by the fact she hasn't seen or heard something already. Thank God she isn't as addicted to her phone as some people. And not only that, eventually we have to go back to work. What happens then?"

Her new job began in a matter of days, and she was well aware that the timing couldn't have been worse. Her father would no sooner be buried than she'd have to get on a plane.

"Logan and Zoey wanted to give Mama time to process things on her own," Dara said, "but time's up. Maybe Zoey should find Mama a counselor?"

"That still won't help us in regard to the funeral." *Or work.* And even though Devon felt guilty for thinking about such things, they were still important aspects that had to be considered.

A sound drew their attention, and Devon shifted

on the couch, turning to see her mother standing in the doorway, looking wild-eyed and panicked. "Mama? Are you all right?"

Her mother's knees buckled, and she went down, catching herself with her hands. Devon and Dara rushed to Rayna Jo's sides, and Devon brushed the hair back from her mother's face. "Mama? Mama, what's wrong?"

Her mother shifted sideways to sit on the floor, and tears streamed down her pale face.

"Talk to us," Devon urged.

"Richard... Richard is *gone*?"

Devon and Dara exchanged a look before Devon nodded. "Yes, Mama, he is."

It took some doing to get her mother up and settled on the couch. While Dara held Rayna Jo, Devon retrieved a damp washcloth. She wanted to pour her mother and herself a stiff drink, but seeing as how she wasn't sure about the alcohol mixing with the medication her mother took for anxiety, Devon promised herself the drink would come later.

"Here," she said, pressing a glass of water into her mother's hands. "Take a sip."

Rayna Jo choked down a swallow of water but then shoved the glass away. "How could he do this to me? After *everything*... how could he do this?"

Dara and Devon snuggled up on either side of their mother and made the appropriate soothing sounds of comfort. "I'm sure he didn't mean to die, Mama," Devon said.

"It's humiliating. That girl... He *promised* me."

Promised her what?

"Mama, what do you mean? Did you know about... her?" Dara asked.

Her mother let loose a sobbing wail.

"Of course I *knew*. I knew about *all* of them."

Devon sucked in a sharp breath and leaned away from her mother, staring at her in shock. "Mama, what do you mean, *all of them*? You mean he... what he was doing was normal?"

Devon watched as her mother wiped her fingers over her eyes before she nodded, head down.

"I confronted him when he first... when I found out. You were both so young. I loved him so *much*. He said none of them mattered. That he did it out of loneliness when he traveled. He s-said he'd stop but... he didn't."

"You stayed with him, though," Dara said.

Fresh tears overflowed and trickled down Rayna Jo's cheeks.

"I made excuses a-and looked the other way. He said he didn't want a divorce, but he'd s-see whomever he liked, whenever he liked, and I had to be okay with it. So I told myself I was."

"Oh, Mama," Devon breathed.

"I-I focused on you girls, and Addy and I opened the shop. Your father and I... had an understanding."

"Did the Babes know?" Dara asked.

Their mother shook her head and sniffled, staring down at her hands. "I don't think so. I never told them. Richard promised he would only see women out of town. He *promised*."

The promise of a cheating man obviously wasn't worth much, Devon thought bitterly. Father or not, his behavior was horrifyingly wrong on so many levels. And the fact that her mother had known? Stayed? That was a level of co-dependence Devon hadn't seen until now. How could she have missed it?

Devon shoved the thought aside because it was too heavy to contemplate at the moment on top of everything else. "Mama, the funeral... We've made the arrangements. Will you be able to handle it?"

CHAPTER SEVEN

The day of the funeral dawned bright and early. Devon watched the sunrise from the sand, noting the small group of locals on the left of the pier who filmed the event with their phones for those not lucky enough to live at the beach.

She watched the short clips every day as she got ready for work, enjoying the devotional the hostess shared to start the day off right.

She wondered what the verse was today. Maybe something on honoring one's spouse. Wouldn't that be ironic.

Devon slid her sunglasses off her head and onto her nose when the sunbeams burst over the horizon and blinded her. And even though she knew she ought to return to the house to get ready for what the day had in store, she couldn't bring herself to stand.

Not when it meant acknowledging the fact she'd never see her father again. Nor was he the man she'd always believed him to be.

Shocked as she was by his behavior, she couldn't paint him as all bad. She'd spent eighteen years in that house, and while her parents had obviously put on a good show for oblivious teenagers focused entirely on themselves, she now saw how flawed they both were.

Ten years had passed since she and Dara had both left home and moved out on their own, but still her mother had stayed. Given that, her mother's co-dependency and her father's narcissistic behavior were the perfect storm for what had taken place, as well as her mother's reaction to her father's death.

"Do you miss it?" a low voice asked from behind her.

She didn't need to turn around to identify the source. "You're up early."

"I'm more productive in the morning after a long walk," Oz said as he lowered himself to the sand beside her.

She didn't turn her head or shift her gaze from the sun streaming over the water.

"So Rayna Jo got her memory back," he said, referring to the text Dara had sent out to the group last night. "How's she doing?"

"I'm not sure," she said honestly. "After the initial rush, she went back to being very quiet."

"She avoided dealing with it at first. Now that she remembers, she has to do it for real."

"I suppose."

"She's not the only one struggling with this."

Oz nudged her side with his elbow.

"Hey. You ever going to look at me?"

She bit back a groan of unease. She'd hoped some time on the sand would calm her nerves for the day ahead. Instead she felt them unraveling even more as she wondered if Ted would attend or not. "What do you want from me, Oz? I've apologized for how I handled things."

"I'm not after an apology, sweetheart."

"So what is it you're after? After all these years, what do you want?"

"Same thing I've always wanted. You."

She sucked in a sharp breath and turned her head toward him so fast a muscle in her neck twinged. "What?"

Oz's blue eyes met hers, and despite her

sunglasses, she felt the intensity all the way to her soul.

"That can't be all that surprising. All I've ever wanted is you, Devon. When are you finally going to see that?"

She opened her mouth to speak, but since she didn't know what to say in response, she snapped it closed and turned her attention back to the surf.

That was why he'd kissed her?

"Okay, you obviously weren't prepared for that revelation, but it doesn't change the truth of it. I didn't chase after you when you left for New York, but it wasn't for lack of wanting to."

"That was ten *years* ago."

"Yes, it was."

"I know you've dated."

"I have," he said simply.

"We aren't the same people."

"Our lifestyles and professions may have evolved, but we are very much the same, I think."

"No. *Every*thing has changed," she said. "I've changed."

"Have you? I still see the same loving, dedicated daughter, sister, and friend you were before you left."

"My life is no longer here. I'm leaving again. I have a job."

"Yes, you do. Temporary morning anchor."

"It's a toe in the door."

"It is," he agreed with a nod. "But what about Rayna Jo?"

Like she could read minds? Predict the future? "You're the one who said no matter what happened, her friends would be there to support her."

"Friends can't replace children."

Which was exactly what she'd told herself a million times since all of this had begun.

She shoved herself to her feet and turned to glare down at him. "Stop."

"Stop what?"

"Pulling a guilt trip on me. I have a life. Dara *has* a life. We can't just rearrange everything because my father couldn't keep it in his pants and my mother was too co-dependent to divorce him years ago."

She turned on her heel and stalked off toward the pier, determined to get away as quickly as possible even though she knew she'd see him in a few hours' time at the service and the gathering afterwards at the house.

But Oz's words had struck a nerve deep within her. After watching her mother collapse beneath the weight of her father's indiscretions, she wondered how long it would be before her mother was strong enough to venture back into the world again.

Back to work?

It wasn't a matter of money. She knew there were insurance policies in place that would provide in the interim, but like Oz had said, her mother needed emotional support.

But with the clock ticking on her time left in Carolina Cove, she knew she either had to return to New York or give up the three-month anchor position. As well as risk never getting another like it again due to what would be seen as a lack of dedication to her career.

But how could she leave with her mother in the state she was in? Dara lived in Wilmington but was currently assigned to a job in Chicago.

Devon jogged up the stairs leading over the dunes and hurried down the wooden planks, every step faster than the one before it.

No one had ever said life would be easy, but *why* did it have to be so complicated?

RAYNA JO TOOK one last look in her floor-length mirror but didn't see herself. The woman staring back looked pale and dark-eyed, the small bit of makeup she'd smeared on doing nothing to hide the shadows and bags beneath her eyes.

No wonder her husband had strayed. Found younger and prettier women to boost his ego. At the moment, she felt ninety-three, not sixty-three. Looked it, too.

Vows are vows.

That they were. And despite the indiscretions, she'd never stopped loving him. But even she knew how strange that was.

"Mama? You ready?" Devon asked.

Rayna Jo turned on the cream tufted vanity stool and faced her eldest daughter. "I'm not sure I can do this."

Devon's expression shifted to one of pity before becoming more determined.

"You can. *We* can. You're not alone, because we are all in this together. God gives us strength to handle the things we think will break us. Isn't that what you've always told us?"

She'd told Devon that in regard to her breakup with Oscar. Because while her daughter had loved Oscar, her desire for New York had pushed them apart, though it hadn't been an easy decision for Devon.

"Let me help you with that," Devon said, coming into the room.

Devon picked up the strand of pearls given to Rayna Jo by her parents on her sweet sixteen, and her daughter placed them around her neck.

"Perfect," Devon said, her hands smoothing over Rayna Jo's shoulders to gently squeeze.

"Are they still outside?" she asked.

"The reporters? One or two. Adam's statement sent most of them away with a few quotes. I think, once the funeral is over, they'll all be gone."

Devon moved to the bed, and Rayna Jo watched in the mirror as her daughter gathered up her purse and the shoes she had yet to put on.

"Mama, we need to leave. Let me help you with these," Devon said, handing over the purse before kneeling in front of Rayna Jo to slip her feet into the plain black pumps she'd chosen.

Rayna Jo felt the shoes slide onto her feet, yet when she shifted her gaze back to the mirror, the image moved eerily in the conversion thing Logan had diagnosed her with before.

She was in the present, very much so, but it still didn't feel quite right. Still felt as though she floated a bit outside of her body.

"Done. Let's go."

Devon urged her up and turned her toward the exit. Along the way, they passed the double doors to Richard's room, and she stumbled. "His gray suit. That's the one he looked best in. I didn't think to ask..."

"Mama, all that's been done. Dara and I took care of it and... we chose a navy suit. It'll be fine."

"Navy," she mused. "Navy did make his eyes look bluer but—" No one would see his eyes. Not ever again. Or the way they would sparkle when he said something ornery. Tease her about being able to cook pretty much anything except oven rolls because she'd burn them each and every time.

Devon's hold on Rayna Jo's arm firmed, and her daughter tugged her along once more. Dara waited at the bottom of the stairs, looking stunning in a simple black dress and flats. Dara wasn't one to wear dresses or heels, but in honor of her father... "You girls look beautiful."

Her voice broke again and Devon patted her hand.

"Come on, Mama. Let's get this done."

A black limo waited outside for them. Rayna Jo and Devon headed toward the car while Dara locked up behind them.

Rayna Jo looked around and saw several

reporters aiming cameras in their direction. She quickly ducked her head and turned her face.

"It's okay, Mama. The worst is almost over," Devon said.

Almost over, she repeated silently.

But was it?

THE SERVICE WAS simple but beautiful. The girls had done a wonderful job with the arrangements. As Rayna Jo sat there observing, she found herself grateful that she hadn't had to make such decisions.

The Babes sat on the row beside and behind her and the girls, their support nearly tangible as people worked their way up the line to pay their last respects.

She'd stood for a while but then woven on her feet, and the girls had made her sit to receive the rest of those gathered. Oliver Beck and his wife were among those in attendance, along with the guard who'd been in the accident that night and his wife.

She was touched by the gesture. That the famous actor would take time out of his day to attend when he undoubtedly had better things to do. Along with getting her memory back, Rayna Jo remembered the details. How Richard had lost control and crossed into oncoming traffic.

The accident was Richard's fault entirely, though the cause of death had been a massive heart attack. As to the other, more sordid details, well, she tried not to think of them.

After a prayer, Oscar made his way to the front of the large room, and those gathered quieted once again as he began to speak into the microphone.

Oscar read the obituary that had been printed in the paper and online, the one stating Richard's age and marital details, family left behind. There was no mention of the poor girl he'd been with when she died or of their relationship.

"...and that's why we're gathered here today," Oscar said in closing. "Out of love for an imperfect man, but most importantly, love for his wife, daughters, and friends. It's a reminder to never take life for granted and to live the type of life that honors those we love. Rayna Jo, Dara, and Devon, on behalf of everyone gathered here, you have our condolences for your loss and our support for the days ahead."

Oh, that boy. Rayna Jo watched as Oscar folded the slip of paper he'd carried to the podium and tucked the paper into his suit pocket as he stepped down.

Leave it to Oscar to find something positive to focus on. On love and the girls. On moving forward.

The funeral director said a few words as well as gave instructions to those going on to the burial at the cemetery.

The director had the family leave first, and as they left the building, cameras sounded from all sides. The girls hurried Rayna Jo into the limo once more.

The ride to the cemetery took about thirty minutes, and during that time, no one spoke. All three of them simply sat there, lost in her own thoughts and emotions.

She didn't doubt the girls were flabbergasted by what they'd discovered, and she promised herself when she was better that she'd make a motherly inquiry into their well-being. But for now, it was too much when she wasn't sure of her own. Her mortification over Richard's behavior left her feeling less of a woman, and all pretense regarding their marriage had been laid bare for the world to see.

They arrived at the plot and waited in their cushioned chairs, staring at the casket while the others parked and made their way to the burial site.

The wind flapped the edges of the tent providing shade, and a few verses were read while single roses were laid atop the casket by Devon and Dara.

Rayna Jo knew she ought to walk up and do the same, at least say goodbye, but she couldn't find the strength to stand. Maybe she'd said her goodbyes a long time ago.

Or maybe she never would.

After one last prayer, people began to wander away. Rayna Jo sat there while others talked in whispers, staring at the casket and the fake green drape over the earth that would cover Richard for eternity.

Was it worth it, his affairs? Had he made his peace before he'd succumbed? Would he face the higher power he'd claimed he believed in without repenting? Face judgment?

Emotions warred within her. Anger and disgust, fear and heartbreak. Agony for the love she'd held for him despite the pain it had brought. You didn't spend forty-two years of your life with someone and not love.

For the first time in her life, she realized she was alone, and her mind whirled with the awareness. She'd gone from her parents' home to marriage and children. Children who now had their own lives to live.

Could she handle being alone? Did she want to be?

"Mama? Mama, it's time to go home."

Home. The house had always been home, but now it seemed beautifully broken. Empty.

The girls grasped each of her arms to prod her up and across the uneven ground, past headstones aged by time and weather.

She walked, though her feet felt as though they belonged to someone else.

"Mrs. Teeks."

Rayna Jo blinked at the man walking toward her. He was young, probably mid-twenties, and dressed far too casually for a funeral. "Yes?"

"What do you want?" Dara asked.

The young man held out an envelope, and Rayna Jo automatically held out a hand to receive it.

"You've been served. I'm sorry for your loss, ma'am."

"Are you freaking *kidding* me?" Dara asked, letting go of Rayna Jo to charge toward the man now backing away. He held his hands up as though in surrender.

"Just doing my job," he said before he turned and hurried back in the direction of the cars parked along the cemetery road.

Dara muttered a few choice words before she stopped and turned to face them. Rayna Jo stared in horror at the envelope in her hand, the law firm's name boldly sprawled across the top.

The Babes, their husbands, and their offspring quickly circled round, but Rayna Jo barely noticed.

"Mama, what is it?" Devon asked.

Rayna Jo watched as Adam Shipley held out a hand, and she gratefully shoved the envelope in his direction.

After a few seconds of reading, Adam looked grim.

"Richard's estate is being sued by the family of the young woman who died in the accident."

"What?"

"Are you serious?"

"Can they do that?"

"Why?"

"How much?" Rayna Jo asked, the words a raw whisper. "What do they want?"

Adam's gaze shifted to hers, and she fought off the urge to be sick because she could tell it was bad.

"Five million dollars."

DEVON HADN'T THOUGHT things could get worse than they already were, but obviously that wasn't true. As they piled into the limo and cars and made their way back to the house, all she could think about was how unfair life was.

Her father was responsible for the accident. For the affair. For the woman's death.

But her mother might lose everything because of it.

How was this possible? What kind of a world made this okay? Where was the justification?

"Well, look who showed up after the fact," Dara muttered.

They'd arrived at the house and gathered their belongings to go in when Devon heard her sister speak.

Devon looked at Dara and then out the window, spotting Ted getting out of a large SUV. Anger filled her. Then something she wasn't sure she could identify since Oz's kiss came to mind, and she wondered if she owed Ted an apology as much as he owed her one. Did a kiss she didn't initiate after telling Ted she was returning his ring qualify as cheating?

No, she decided. It didn't.

"Who is that?" Rayna Jo asked.

"Ted," Devon said. "He's my... It's Ted, Mama."

The door to the limo opened, and Devon surged out, remembering her manners enough to thank the driver before forcibly taking slow steps toward the man she'd given up hope of seeing.

She wanted to rush, to race into his arms and have him hold her, comfort her like a man who loved her would, but something held her back. A combination of anger and guilt and all the emotions ranging between the two. "You're here," she said simply when she got within speaking distance.

"I am. I went to the burial, but I arrived late and didn't want to make a scene walking up to the gravesite."

He'd been there? She didn't stop but kept walking, leaving it up to him whether or not he followed.

Devon unlocked the door and entered the house.

"Devon?"

So he had followed her. "I'm going up to change. Wait there." She knew Ted hated being told anything, but the last thing she wanted was for him to follow her up the stairs to the privacy of her bedroom when she needed time to sort through her emotions.

It was rude not to introduce him to her family now that he'd made the trip, but in her upset, she needed a few minutes to decompress.

She changed out of the too hot black dress and into a pair of tan capris and a moss-green sleeveless top, adding a pair of wedges since it would be rude to walk around barefoot with guests in the house.

She paused at the top of the stairs when she saw Ted staring at a photo of her family. Then the door opened and Oz entered and paused.

Oz was an inch or so shorter than Ted, but he was broader of shoulder and seemingly more fit. Her comparison didn't stop there, though. For the first time, she noticed Ted's handsome face held a pretty-boy slant whereas Oz's was more blunt and masculine.

You're sounding petty, Dev.

"Can I help you?" Oz asked.

Ted turned and flashed his camera-ready smile.

"He's with me," Devon said, drawing both men's attention to her as she began her descent. "Theodore George, Oscar Roman."

"The novelist," Ted said. "Devon said you were a friend of the family."

"Yes," Oz said, his gaze shifting from Ted to her.

Devon got a bit flustered beneath the force of it and cleared her throat. "Oz, Ted and I need a moment. Would you mind telling Dara she'll have to do without me for a while?"

"Of course," Oz said.

He dipped his head and gave her a look that reminded her of the kiss on the beach and the chemistry still very present between them. She instinctively knew his thoughts, knew he challenged her to own up to her warring feelings for him despite the ring she now held in her hand.

Oz had no sooner left than the door opened again, and Michael and Logan entered. They also stopped when they saw the two of them together.

"You must be Ted," Logan said, extending his hand. "I'm Devon's cousin Logan, and this is my brother, Michael."

Introductions made, Devon excused them and prodded Ted down the hallway toward her father's study before the door could open and more of her extended family could arrive.

"Nice house," Ted said, moving across the study to take a look at the oceanfront view outside.

Even though her father was rarely home, he'd insisted on his home office having the view rather than the living area more often used by them all.

"I didn't think you were coming," she said.

He swung around, expression tight.

"My attendance was mandatory—or so I surmised from your voicemail."

She blinked at his tone and crossed her arms over her front, the ring burning against her palm. "I was angry when I left that message. I'm sorry," she said, "but I also meant what I said about returning the ring. I desperately needed you here for the service and burial. For comfort and support."

"I'm here now."

Her entire body felt like it was a bow string pulled taut. "Yes, you are. Now that the reporters have gone, the service is *over*, and your constituents won't see you."

Ted muttered a low curse and moved toward her.

"I tried to get here for the service, Devon. The fog was soup-thick this morning, and we couldn't take off on time. I tried, though. You can check our flight log and the delay. Doesn't that count for something?"

She stared at him, reading the truth in his expression.

"You know that I love you. I care about you. I just couldn't get here in time, Devon."

She inhaled, closed her eyes, and nodded. "I believe you."

He brushed a kiss over her forehead, his hands sliding down her arms to hers. When he encountered her closed fist, he glanced at her again.

"I brought it to give back to you," she said. "With everything going on I think maybe we should wait." She opened her hand and revealed the beautiful ring.

Ted cradled her hand in one of his while plucking the ring from her.

"You've expressed your thoughts very clearly, Ted. But my father... This mess... I can't ignore it, especially now. My mother's being sued," she told him. "So the press and attention aren't over yet. It's just beginning."

She watched as Ted grimaced at the news and her heart pinched. "You didn't see the man serve her after the burial?"

"No. I left when everyone else did."

"I see."

"Look, Devon, I know you're still upset with me, but don't overthink this and make it out to be more than it is."

Overthink it? More than it was? "Ted, I *needed* you today. I needed you to be by my side, holding my hand, *supporting* me. If you're going to pick and choose and shy away from the bad and only be around for the good... that's not the way to start a marriage."

He reached out and grasped her arms, running his hands up and down the lengths.

"I know. I'm sorry. You have to realize this is uncharted waters for me here, too. Devon, the future I'm trying to protect is for both of us. Can't you see that?"

"I do. I really do understand, but my father *died*," she said. "My mother hasn't been in her right mind due to the stress of it, and Dara and I have been scrambling to keep things together. You could've helped us. Helped me."

He drew her close and hugged her, and she felt his lips brush over her temple.

"I'm here now. Can't we focus on that?"

She buried her face against his chest and willed herself to let go of her disappointment. If he said he'd tried to make it, he had. He didn't control the weather... even if he could've left the night before and avoided the morning fog. "How long are you staying?"

"We're leaving this afternoon."

She tensed and lifted her head. "What? What do you mean, *we*?"

"Did you forget? Devon, we have the gala tonight and a fundraising luncheon for my campaign tomorrow."

"Ted, I can't... You want me to go to events like that? *Now?*"

"It'll help you move forward," Ted said, his tone soft. "We can put this mess with your father behind us. Not to mention, as previous commitments, you can use them as an excuse to get away from all of the drama here."

"Ted—"

"You know you'll need to clear your head before you start work Monday morning. The events will get you back in the groove of things. Back to real life."

Real life? "This is pretty real," she muttered.

But his words centered her mind on work. On starting the new job the day after tomorrow. The days had flown by so quickly she'd actually lost track.

"We'll spend an hour or so here, get you packed, and be on our way," Ted said. "And this," he said, taking the ring from her hand, "can go back on your finger tonight once we're back in New York and things have settled. Okay?"

"Dev? *Devon!*" Dara called from somewhere in the house.

Devon pulled away from Ted and hurried toward the door, the panic in Dara's voice spurring her on. "In the study," she called back as she yanked open the door. "What's wrong?"

Footsteps rang through the foyer, and Devon watched as her sister skidded a bit in her rush before she came running down the hallway.

"Mom's gone."

"What? What do you mean, gone?"

"Gone, like *gone* gone. We can't find her anywhere. Have you seen her?"

CHAPTER EIGHT

When Rayna Jo left the house, she didn't have a destination in mind. She simply had to get away from the pitying looks from her best friends, away from the crush of loved ones who offered support yet suffocated her in the process.

Far, far away from the memories and the life she had built with a man who'd ultimately destroyed her in the process of destroying himself.

Maybe most importantly, she wanted to escape the awareness that Devon followed in her footsteps, and her heart had shattered at the sadness she saw in her daughter's future.

Some women were made to be a politician's wife.

They were fine never being a priority because the office and responsibilities came first. Those women were the public face of the man being encouraged to move up in the world while being told to mind her place, a pretty face in the background for photo ops.

And as she'd made her way to the downstairs powder room, she'd overheard them talking in the den. Listened to her daughter speak of needing her fiancé at her side while Ted smoothly talked his way out with excuses.

Just like Richard had done.

Rayna Jo *knew* in her heart that Devon would never be truly happy with Ted.

Devon deserved love, to be a priority. She deserved respect so that she didn't find herself sixty-three and broken by the man she loved.

Rayna Jo glanced down at the legal papers on the seat beside her, wondering why she'd brought them when the whole point was to run away from all of it.

She knew the answer though.

By bringing the papers, she kept herself grounded in the here and now. In the darkness of reality and the pain wreaking havoc on her emotions, bringing back the fogginess from before.

A horn blared, and she jerked the wheel to bring

the car back into her lane. She found herself driving toward a favorite spot where she liked to sit and watch the sunset.

The location drew her with its comforting familiarity, and she slowed when she approached the end of the island, forcing herself to watch for people or unattended children walking a little too far into the road.

She found a place to park and sat there, the AC blowing in her face like an arctic wind.

People circled round in convertibles and Jeeps and other vehicles, locals and tourists alike simply out for a drive on a beautiful day.

A truck backed a boat down the ramp toward the water, and in the distance, kite surfers swooped up in the air with every blast of the ocean breeze.

They looked carefree, while she felt herself buckling inch by inch, breaking from the weight she carried.

Five *million* dollars.

Even if the family of the woman would agree to settle, it would undoubtedly cost her the house, her half of the business.

She'd prayed for the day her grandchildren would run laughing through the downstairs on their way to the beach, and instead, it would belong to strangers.

Or God forbid, someone would buy it and create a rental, changing over week after week. It wouldn't be the home her parents had built on a lot later divided so that Adaline and her husband could build and live there as well.

Rayna Jo watched a group of pelicans flying overhead. One left the group and swooped down, circling, until it landed atop a kayak on a trailer parked in front of her.

As though sensing her stare, the pelican seemingly made eye contact, and a feeling of disbelief rushed over Rayna Jo.

The bird flapped its wings, still looking in her direction. Her gaze shifted to the kayak left behind by a local company, and even though she knew it was wrong and she'd undoubtedly get into trouble, she opened the door and got out, more than a little conspicuous in her black dress and pumps.

What could they do? Sue her?

Get in line.

The late-afternoon heat blasted her as she crossed the asphalt, and once behind the truck and trailer, she was hidden from view except for those on the water side too busy to pay her any mind.

She set about unhooking the kayak, aware that the pelican watched her every move from its perch. Silently encouraging?

"What am I doing?" she muttered to herself.

The pelican blinked and stayed put until the last tie was loosened and then hopped into flight and flew to the railing mere steps away by the kayak launch.

Rayna Jo felt as though the bird led her through the steps, and even though she'd never stolen anything in her life, she hefted the kayak off the trailer as though it were hers and managed to drag it to the launch, thankful the truck had parked in the spot directly beside it.

She left it on the edge of the launch and went back for the paddle, and once she had it in hand, the pelican hopped off the railing into the water, floating gracefully at the bow bobbing with the gentle waves.

Still, the bird faced Rayna Jo, its beady eyes watching.

Waiting?

She didn't let herself think beyond the moment, the mini goals that drove her.

Get the kayak off the trailer.

Get the kayak in the water.

Get away from the shore and people and her life.

Whatever happened then would happen. Whatever happened... would be for the best.

She bit back a hysterical laugh and told herself she'd really lost her mind this time. But she felt compelled by a force she couldn't shake.

Rayna Jo took off her shoes and tossed them into the seat, then shoved off and splashed through calf-deep water as she climbed aboard and settled into the cockpit, shoving her shoes into the hatch for safe-keeping.

She'd kayaked with Richard and the twins, as well as the Babes, many times over the years, so she wasn't a novice.

Rayna Jo paddled out atop the waves pushing her back toward shore. Finally she made it, and then... she just kept paddling, every dip propelling her farther down the Cape Fear River.

She used the foot braces to steer the boat along the shore, grateful no one paid her any attention as she slowly paddled along.

The pelican floated beside her for quite some time, but after a while, it spread its wings and took flight, landing on the bow of her stolen kayak like a figurehead on a boat born for the sea.

At one point, she became vaguely aware of the ferry to Southport on her starboard side, but she ignored it and kept going, past Zeke's Island and No Name Island on her port side, down the river toward the sea.

She'd never kayaked so far on her own before, but the current made it easy. She mostly navigated, steering clear of the channels through the nature preserve for fear of snakes and alligators or whatever else might be lurking there and sticking to the outside edge of the river.

The sound of the wind and lapping waves calmed her nerves as the sun set, and her mind filled with a haziness that tempered the raw, painful edges of awareness.

Every stroke of the paddle, the sound of the water drops plopping when she lifted one end to slide the other down... She lost herself in maintaining the slow pace, unwilling to stop even though she had no destination in mind.

The current carried her along and greatly aided her efforts, pushing her farther south toward Bald Head Island.

So she just kept paddling, getting closer and closer to the Atlantic with every stroke—and more and more willing to let the current and the pelican lead her wherever they wanted.

IT TOOK everything in Oz to keep his mouth shut and pretend to be oblivious to the fact Devon's boyfriend had actually showed up. Didn't she realize the guy was a louse?

He sat outside in the beautifully landscaped backyard at the Teekses', his mind reeling from the latest fallout from Richard's accident.

Five million dollars. He knew Richard and Rayna Jo were fairly well off, but he'd be hard-pressed to believe they had that kind of money. Even with any life insurance policies that might have been issued.

"Hey," Michael called from the house. "Have you seen Rayna Jo?"

Oz turned and shook his head. "No, not out here."

He heard some commotion in the house and got up to go check it out. Inside he heard various members of the family and friends calling Rayna Jo's name and doors being opened and shut rapidly. "What's going on?"

Michael was a step away from the large kitchen pantry when he paused long enough to slide Oz a worried look.

"She's missing," Michael said.

"The rental's gone!" Dara called from the front of the house before a door slammed. "Mama must have taken it."

Without a word, the group assembled en masse in the foyer of the large home, everyone speaking at once.

"Her purse is upstairs," Adaline said, hurrying down the stairs. "I checked her bedroom, the kitchen, the spare rooms—everywhere."

Devon stood across the foyer from Oz, Ted a step behind her, looking irritated at the chaos erupting around him.

Oz fought the urge to plant his fist in the man's face.

"Should we call the police?" Mary Elizabeth asked, wringing her hands in front of her.

"I'm sure that's not necessary," Ted said. "She probably just needed some air."

"Considering her emotional state of late, yes," Logan said, disagreeing with the man. "Yes, we should call. Immediately."

"Oh, Logan, surely you don't think she'd—" Adaline broke off, glancing at Dara and Devon, unable to finish the sentence even though her expression said it all.

"I hope not," Logan said, "but better to call the police now so they can be looking."

"I'll do that," Adam Shipley said, leaving the group. "Dara, what's the make and model of the rental car? Do you know the license plate number?"

Dara headed off with Adam to get the information.

"We can drive around and look, but if she's in a vehicle, she could be anywhere," Michael said. "Especially since we're not sure how long she's been gone. Are there any favorite spots she might go to?"

Oz watched as the Babes exchanged glances.

"She likes the state park," Mary Elizabeth said. "Down by the marina."

"Or the south end of the island," Adaline said.

"The pier, too," Cheryl Dummit added.

"She could walk to the pier. She wouldn't have to take the rental," Devon said.

"No, but given her mindset, she might not be thinking clearly," Logan said.

"I'll go to the state park," Michael said. "Oz, you head to the south end. Dara and Devon can go to the pier. Logan, you check the boardwalk. Mom, you and Dad stay here in case she comes back or if the police come by. Everyone else just spread out and search."

Oz watched as Adaline turned toward her husband, and the quiet man hugged her close. Hubert Davenport wasn't the most talkative man, but he had always been a stable presence in his family's lives.

Tessa and her daughters headed out the door on foot, while Mary Elizabeth's girls agreed to take Allie's minivan to accommodate her kids while driving about the neighborhood.

"What about us?" Hadley asked Logan.

Oz hadn't had much contact with Cheryl and Jerry Dummit's daughter over the years, but since her divorce, she'd moved back to town and currently dated a local contractor. The two seemed happy—really happy—and more than eager to help.

"I honestly don't know," Logan said to them. "Just drive until someone finds her. The moment someone knows something, get a text out to the rest of us and we'll meet back here."

Oz turned toward the door to leave when he saw Devon arguing with Ted. He couldn't hear what was being said, but their expressions revealed whatever it was wasn't good.

He focused on the task Logan had given him and headed out the door, glad the reporters had finally taken a break now that the funeral was over and weren't witnessing the chaos erupting due to Rayna Jo's disappearance.

Still, had they been there, maybe one of them would've noticed Rayna Jo leaving. Figured that, when they'd be useful, they weren't.

"Wait!"

He turned at the sound of Devon's voice and saw her running to catch up with him.

"Can I go with you?"

"I thought you were heading to the pier with Dara?"

"Dara's still going, but there's no reason for Mama to drive there."

"Uh, yeah, okay. Are we... waiting for Ted?" The last thing he wanted to do was make small talk with the man under the circumstances.

Devon walked past him and kept going toward the truck he'd parked down the street to give the family members plenty of room in the driveway.

"No."

No? "He's not helping with the search?"

"Not unless he sees her at the airport," she muttered dryly.

Oz fell into step beside of her. "Want to talk about it?"

"No."

"Your call." They kept walking, and at the fast pace she'd set, they reached his truck in seconds. He hit the key fob and opened the passenger door for her, hurrying around the front to climb behind the wheel while fuming at the fact the guy had abandoned her again.

He jabbed the key in the ignition and got them in motion.

"You're upset," she said softly. "I can tell."

"I'm worried about your mom. What's his excuse this time?"

"He... He has to return to New York tonight. He couldn't stay and help."

"Couldn't—or didn't want to?"

"You know nothing about our relationship, Oz."

"So you've said before."

"He's an important man, all right? He has to be there for a gala that's being held in his honor. *I'd promised* to be there with him, but now that my mother is missing—"

"Poor guy had to leave you here to handle it alone? Sucks for him," he said, unable to keep the derision from his tone.

He glanced across the interior and found her

gaze quickly shifting from him to the window beside her.

"It's complicated," she said. "You wouldn't understand."

"No, I guess it is beyond my comprehension, because to me, a fiancé or boyfriend or whatever you're calling him today should be by your side during times like this. Nothing is more important than you and Rayna Jo and Dara right now."

Devon yanked on her seat belt to readjust it at her neck and gripped it in her fist.

Oz glanced down and glared at the rockless finger on her hand. Even though it wasn't there, it was. Binding her to someone who didn't appreciate her. She knew her own mind, always had. Did he have it wrong? Had she changed that much?

"Finding Mama is the only thing that matters now. Let's focus on that."

Love is blind. Wasn't that the saying? he mused, shooting a glance her way before turning his attention to the road in front of him.

Blind, deaf, and dumb, he added, wondering how a man could be so stupid as to think anything more important than family.

Devon's return couldn't have had worse timing. He'd been pondering life a lot of late, thinking it was about time he found someone to create a life with. Maybe have children?

But after seeing her again, he knew he'd have to start over when it came to forgetting her. Because until he managed it, he didn't want to treat a woman as second best, which was exactly the way Ted treated Devon.

The traffic leaving the beach had thickened as people headed home for dinner. Oz fought his impatience with the slow-moving vehicles.

The two-lane road to the end of the island was crowded as well, but with no lights to impede the pace, it was a straight shot. He still had to watch for cops, pedestrians, and bicyclists, but they finally made it.

"There! That's the rental," Devon said, pointing toward the left as they slowly drove through the parking area.

Oz stopped behind the vehicle and they both hurried out.

"Mama?" Devon called.

Oz rushed to the driver's side while Devon went to the passenger door. The driver's door opened, and he pressed the button to unlock the rest. "Let's look around," he said to Devon after a glance into the backseat.

Devon grabbed the papers and envelope left on the passenger seat and turned to survey their surroundings. "Ma—uh, Rayna Jo!"

He pulled out his phone and texted the group to let them know they'd found the rental and where. The police were next, and by then, he and Devon had walked the area from end to end, looking for any sign of her and asking the people they found if they'd seen a woman matching the picture of Rayna Jo Devon had on her phone.

The police arrived and Oz waited impatiently while they checked out the vehicle and the same paths Oz and Devon had already searched.

The area was crowded with people. Tourists cruising through, fishermen, boaters coming back after a day on the water. Surely someone had seen something?

Devon paced the asphalt, a phone to her ear and undoubtedly Dara on the other end of the call.

One of the policemen approached Oz.

"No sign of her. We've issued an alert, and the Coast Guard is asking boaters to keep an eye out."

"You think she's on the water?" Devon asked in obvious surprise.

Oz noted the man looked extremely uncomfortable with the question, and Oz had a good idea of why.

Given Rayna Jo's mental state and the news she'd received, she wouldn't be the first person to commit suicide due to emotional and financial ruin.

"We're just trying to get as many eyes searching for her as possible, ma'am," the policeman said. "We'll be in touch if we hear anything."

Oz thanked the man and his partner for their help and then closed the distance between him and Devon, tugging her into his arms and holding her close, his chin atop her head. "We're going to find her."

"Alive?" Devon asked, the word muffled against his dress shirt.

He kissed her hair and squeezed her a bit tighter. "We'll find her."

Several seconds passed, but Devon slowly wrapped her arms around his waist, hands at the base of his back.

"Thank you."

"No thanks needed."

"No, there is. Thank you for being here, for being my friend."

Friend? He supposed he was that, even though he'd never stopped wanting to be more.

"What else is going to go wrong?"

His thriller writer's mind could think of all too many possibilities, few of them with a happy ending. So he kissed her head and remained silent, hoping the question was rhetorical.

"Where is she, Oz? Where did she go?"

CHAPTER NINE

Devon hated everything about the day. The reporters and funeral, the stress of Ted's arrival. Her mother's disappearance.

From start to finish, it had gone from bad to worse to catastrophic.

Now she sat on the porch watching the moon rise above the Atlantic, unable to sleep because it was dark and her mother had yet to be found.

Where *was* she? Where had she gone without her purse? Money? Bank cards? A vehicle?

Don't go there.

She didn't want to consider the horrible alternative, but seeing as how they'd found the rental car at the end of the island... how could she not?

Ted had contacted her once he'd landed to ask if she'd been found, but the conversation had been short and stilted. His handler assistant had called regarding a problem with the gala's security, and Ted had quickly said goodbye. It was another smack in the face after a devastating day.

"Can't sleep?" Oz said.

She'd been so lost in thought she hadn't heard the door open, nor Oz's exit onto the porch.

"You should try to rest, Devon. Logan might have something that would help."

She inhaled a shuddering breath and shook her head. "No. I don't want to take anything. Not when I don't know where she is. If she's... still with us."

Everyone had eventually made it back to the house after searching their designated locations and the surrounding areas. The island wasn't that big when it came to spots her mother liked to visit, but it seemed Rayna Jo had simply vanished.

No one wanted to leave the house in case there was news, but the Babes had eventually gone home since they literally lived within shouting distance, and they'd taken their adult children with them to sleep in real beds before the search resumed again in the morning.

Logan, Michael, Oz, as well as Tessa's daughter,

Lily, had all stayed behind to keep Dara and Devon company during their vigil, while Zoey had to work.

"Scoot over," Oz said.

He'd said the words while literally on the way down to the couch beside her, and she scrambled sideways to give him more room. Oz had brought a throw with him, and once he was settled, he draped the blanket around her to combat the cool night breeze.

"Thanks."

"You're welcome. Look, Devon—"

"Don't say it." She shook her head, unable to look at him. "Don't say everything will be okay. You don't know that."

"You're right. I don't know that. But I do know no matter what happens, *you* will be all right. You're not alone."

But she was. Ted was gone, unable to be there due to his campaign schedule and fear of scandal. And if she didn't report to work tomorrow morning as she was supposed to, her career would be gone as well.

She had about a twelve-hour window left given the time it would take to get back to New York.

But how could she do that with her mother

missing and so much going on here? What kind of person would that make her?

Her stomach knotted up like a giant stone. She drew her legs up and wrapped her arms around her knees, hugging them tight.

Her mother wasn't the only one losing everything. Or feeling the devastating fallout. *Mama, come home.*

Oz inhaled and exhaled loudly.

"Don't freak out when I do this," he said.

"Do what?"

He shifted on the couch, the arm at her back from when he'd wrapped the throw around her firming as he scooped her up and transferred her onto his lap.

"Oz."

"I'm cold," he said too quickly. "You need to share the blanket."

She stayed stiff and unyielding for all of five seconds before she gave in to the warmth of his body and the need to be held, comforted, and tucked her forehead into his neck.

She cuddled up against his broad chest and took shallow breaths in an attempt to stem the sobs threatening to erupt because of the show of kindness. "Why are you doing this?"

"Doing what?"

"Being so... nice to me. You should hate me." She felt his lips against her hair, her forehead.

"Would you rather I be mean?"

"Yes."

"Really?"

"It's just a lot to process. Along with everything else."

"I guess if it helps you—pretend I'm Ted."

She tilted her head back on his upper arm. "Never."

"I don't have that pretty-boy look, huh?"

"Stop." She lifted her fingers to his face, his chin, and the light stubble. "You know how handsome you are."

She shifted against him, her eyes growing heavy as his warmth and the blanket left her feeling cozy. Her exhaustion kicked in, and she struggled to remember why letting Oz hold her was a bad idea.

Oz's heartbeat pounded soothingly beneath her ear, and she found herself matching the rise and fall of his chest as he breathed. "Oz?"

"Mmm?"

"Don't take my cooperation as encouragement," she mumbled around a stifled yawn.

"Wouldn't dream of it."

"I am sorry, you know," she whispered, giving up the effort it took to keep her eyes open. "I hate that I hurt you."

"You weren't ready. It would've hurt worse to have found out after the fact and ended up fighting because of it."

It was true. She'd grown up a lot in New York. Having never been on her own or lived away from home, she'd faced a lot of realities her spoiled self hadn't faced until that point.

Oz gently tightened his hold, and with the squeeze, more of her tension faded.

She knew she ought to protest his holding her. Get up, go to bed. Alone. Ted would be angry if he saw them like this and for good reason.

But the thought of moving and the effort involved were too much for her exhausted body to consider, and she sank a bit deeper into Oz's warmth.

Ted couldn't be angry when he should've been there. Should've been the one holding her, comforting her, supporting her. The fact that he wasn't left her asking herself if she was really okay with his decisions. Not only to fly back to New York but... others.

Was she letting fear and stress cloud her feelings for him? Maybe. But what about their future? The upsets and problems to come? Would she face them alone as well?

The man holding her pressed his lips to her hair, and she forced her lashes up, her head back.

"Thank you," she murmured.

"For what?"

"Being my friend."

Oz stared down at her with an expression she recognized but couldn't acknowledge.

"I'll always be your friend."

The words meant more to her than he'd ever know. She inhaled, breathing in Oz's scent, one of man and musk and spice along with the salt air and that intrinsically undefinable headiness that made Oz Oz.

Unease settled deep within her as awareness dawned.

She was upset because Ted had chosen his career over her—which was exactly what she had done to Oz.

Was this her payback? Life's way of showing her how it felt?

She didn't like it. Maybe because... it left her wanting more?

"HELLO. BEAUTIFUL MORNING, ISN'T IT?"

Rayna Jo blinked and looked up at the man standing over her on the beach, but since he stood with his back to the blinding sunrise, she couldn't make out much more than his shadow. She'd been so deep in thought she hadn't noticed his approach.

She'd paddled until she couldn't lift her arms for another stroke. Then she'd floated with the current, not caring where she wound up.

She'd roused when she heard the distinct sound of ocean waves and felt the current getting stronger. And no matter how badly she wanted to let it take her out to sea, something inside of her had demanded she beach the kayak and find the courage to live. Fight. For her daughters.

For herself.

No matter what the future might hold.

"I didn't mean to startle you. Are you okay?" the man asked, not getting the hint that she didn't want to talk when she hadn't responded to his first question.

She nodded and forced herself to communicate. "Fine."

"Did you sleep on the beach?"

Given what she no doubt looked like, she'd think

the answer obvious. "I-I got lost kayaking. I needed to wait until dawn to get my bearings."

"I see. Good thing you did or you'd have been in the Atlantic," the man said, confirming her thoughts as he squatted down in front of her. "It's just that way a little farther. No offense, now, but you look mature enough to know better than to get lost on the water. Mighty dangerous."

She nodded and forced herself to meet his gaze, finding the man to be her age, with warm blue eyes and a head full of silver-white hair and only hints of dark remaining. "It couldn't be helped."

"I see. I'm Connor. Connor Sennet. What's your name?"

"Rayna," she said, leaving off her middle name for reasons she didn't know.

Maybe... Maybe because Rayna Jo was that woman who'd accepted her husband's behavior and wanted to disappear into the sea.

While Rayna—

Rayna battled the currents and the bugs and the night and the danger. Even more, Rayna battled the darkness of her mind and the fog threatening to overtake her yet again—only this time she'd won.

"Well, Miss Rayna, my house is behind you. I

saw you sitting down here for a while and thought I'd check on you. How would you like some breakfast?"

"No, thank you. I couldn't possibly—"

"It'd be my pleasure." His smile coaxed her. "I've never found a mermaid on the beach. The least I can do is feed her breakfast."

A mermaid?

She blushed, knowing how utterly horrible she must look after her night of crying and anger and finally tearful acceptance that nothing was in her control. It never had been. "Maybe I could use your phone? To call my family."

The man smiled at her again, and the sunrise highlighted the little crinkles around his eyes as he extended a hand to help her up, standing with her. Once on her feet, she saw the way he frowned at her clothing. Yeah, a black dress wasn't exactly what one wore to kayak in.

"You look a little overdressed, Rayna."

She attempted to pat the sand from her skirt and shrugged. "I suppose I am. I left in a hurry because... I needed to clear my head. My husband died."

"I see."

She glanced at him again and found the same pitying expression that had sent her scurrying out of the house yesterday. "While with his twenty-three-year-old mistress," Rayna added, just for shock effect.

It worked, because Connor's dark eyebrows flew high on his forehead, and he lifted a hand to rub over his mouth as he tried to hide another grin. He had a handsome, easy smile.

"Well, now, I suppose if that had been the case, I'd need some time to myself, too. My wife passed a few years back. Cancer, not cheating."

A huff of a laugh left her because of their inane conversation, and she shook her head with a wry groan. "I'm sorry. I suppose I shouldn't have blurted it out like that. It's just I'm *sick* of everyone looking at me with the pitying expression you just had."

"Ahh, yes," he said, nodding his head several times. "I remember that expression. My apologies," he said, bowing slightly at the waist. "Won't happen again. Shall we?"

Rayna smoothed her sand-coated hands over her damp dress to try to rid herself of some of the grit before giving up. Live at the beach and sand was a fact of life. Sleep on the beach and it was a lost cause.

Connor extended a hand toward her left, and she turned in that direction. The man fell into step beside her before she stopped once more. "The kayak. I should—"

"Allow me." Connor returned to where she'd sat and hefted the kayak. Rayna picked up the paddle and her arms felt like lead noodles as she dragged it along, reminding her of the strength of the current and just how much danger she'd placed herself in.

Thankfully the walkway to his house wasn't too far from them, and the moment they were on the wooden path winding over the dunes to his home, he set the kayak down.

"It'll be safe here. Nobody'll bother it."

"You're not even winded," she said, leaning on the paddle as she gasped for breath coming up the soft sand incline.

He smiled at her and shrugged. "When my wife was sick, I discovered it helped to take my frustration out on gym equipment. It helped me cope."

"I should try it. I haven't been to a gym in ages," she said, feeling very old and out of shape.

"You're just hungry. Come on," Connor urged. "We'll get you fixed right up."

She followed him up the narrow walkway to a gorgeous two-story house. It sat on a hill about an eighth of a mile from shore, a sprawling, stately looking home with turret-like balconies, walls of windows, and a view that had to be amazing. "It's beautiful."

"Thank you. My wife was an architect."

"My nephew is an architect," she said, trying to add to the conversation.

The closer they got to the house, the more awkward it felt to be accompanying a stranger, much less a man she'd met only minutes ago. "I'm a mess. Would you mind bringing out the phone?"

"Nonsense. Come in," he insisted. "If you're worried about your safety, I promise to keep my distance."

"I could be the crazy one," she said, thinking of the past week and her stress-induced amnesia. That qualified as crazy, right?

Last night on the water, she'd had to fight off the fugue state. She found herself drifting in and out, aware of what she was doing and then... not. It was terrifying.

Not panicking had become a priority, and as she'd continued along and decided life was worth living and her girls deserved better than to lose their mother, too, the fog had slowly faded.

"Oh, I'm pretty good at reading people. I'll take my chances," Connor said, drawing her attention back to him as he moved to a door and unlocked it by pressing a series of numbers.

They entered into an open living area with a

kitchen at the far end. "Oh, it's gorgeous," she breathed, her exhaustion sliding away as her interior design side surged briefly to life.

"I hope so. That means it'll fetch a good price. I'm thinking of selling it."

She turned to look at him in surprise and watched as he shrugged.

"The whole plan was to retire here with my wife, but she died before the house was finished. I've found it to be lonely rambling around in it now."

Her heart pinched at the sadness she saw, heard. What would it be like to be loved so much? "How long ago did your wife pass?"

"Two years."

And he still mourned. That was love.

"Your husband died recently?" he asked with a nod toward her black dress and a lift of one thick eyebrow.

"A few days ago. The... funeral was yesterday."

"That's tough to handle, no matter the circumstances. Please, have a seat. Would you like some coffee?"

"Oh, yes. Thank you." She lifted a hand to brush the hair out of her face and noted how grimy it looked. "But I really shouldn't stay. I'm getting sand everywhere," she said, spotting the trail of sand she left with every step.

"Would you like a shower?"

The question surprised her so much she wasn't sure what to think. Was he merely being neighborly and kind, or—

"You have nothing to fear from me, hon. Scout's honor."

"Were you really a scout?" she asked, gaze narrowed on him.

A husky chuckle rumbled from his chest.

"I was," he said. "Come on, let me show you the guest room, and then I'll fix us some food before taking you back to your family."

Wary though desperate for some hot water to rid herself of sand as well as wake her exhausted body up, she followed him through the house to another section separated by a large room with a pool table and some pinball machines.

"The guest rooms," he said, opening a door. "Totally private. Feel free to use all the locks," he said. "There are some clothes in the closets and drawers. My daughter-in-law leaves them behind so she doesn't have to pack them here every trip. You look about her size, so something should fit. Help yourself."

"That's very kind. I can't thank you enough."

"No problem. Towels are in the closet in the bathroom. Help yourself to whatever else you need. I'll be in the kitchen when you're finished."

She walked with him toward the door and watched as Connor left.

Her hands trembled with fatigue and her overwrought emotions. She shut the door with a quiet click and then twisted the lock, then took it a step further and wrangled an armchair over and shoved it beneath the doorknob.

One couldn't be too careful these days, and at least the noise would alert her to anyone trying to get in.

That done, she moved to the closet. Inside were a couple of sundresses, three pair of capris, two simple tops, and a couple of T-shirts. There were also polos, a few men's dress shirts, and slacks.

A look inside the dresser drawers revealed underwear much too young for her taste, as well as several pairs of shorts, bathing suits, and in a different drawer, there were underwear, swim trunks, and socks suitable for a younger man.

Connor's son?

She helped herself to one of the more modest

sundresses and undergarments and carried them to the bathroom, pausing a moment to take it in.

The room was gorgeously done with flowing marble tile, a soaking tub she longed to use, and a walk-in shower with a built-in seat and rainfall shower head as well as multiple jets on the walls.

The vanity was large and spacious, and out of curiosity, she opened the drawers there as well and found tinted moisturizer, sunscreen, aftershave, toothpaste, and a package of disposable razors.

Exploration completed, Rayna turned on the shower and stripped while it warmed. Towels were in the closet where Connor had said they'd be, and she got what she needed before moving into the walk-in.

"Thank You, Lord," she breathed, welcoming the water and the warmth and the comfort it brought.

She stood in front of the multiple sprays for a long, long time, simply letting them blast her until she forced herself to scrub away the sand and salt and grime and then lathered her hair.

A few tears intermixed with the water, but they were born of exhaustion rather than grief. She'd determined during her time on the beach that she'd shed the last tears she'd cry for Richard. She was simply too tired to care what happened at this point.

Out of my control, she reminded herself.

All that mattered now was that she was safe and clean.

And honestly—still alive.

God's plan for her would play out as it was meant to, and while she certainly couldn't comprehend the whys and hows or the fact she was now being sued for millions of dollars, she had to accept that it was somehow part of the process.

She nodded, determined to give up the worry and focus on the moment and what she could control. Even if it was something as simple as the temperature of the water, which scented shampoo she decided to use, or whether or not she shaved her legs.

Rayna rinsed her hair and then tried to clean the mess of sand she'd left in the shower. Her curly hair had always been troublesome in the south's humidity, but thankfully it required little fixing as a result. She left it free to dry and used the clip she'd worn to the funeral to pull the sides back from her face.

Twenty minutes after blocking the door, she moved the chair back to its original position and made her way through the quiet house to the kitchen, footsteps dragging. She'd wanted so badly to curl up on the guest bed and nap. Moving was her way to stay awake at this point.

Connor saw her coming and lifted the television remote to quickly turn off the TV.

"Feel better?" he asked as she entered the kitchen.

"Yes, thank you. I hope your daughter-in-law doesn't mind me borrowing her things. I'll launder them and return them."

Connor smiled and nodded. "She'd be happy to help. Sit down. You're just in time. We can eat here or out on the patio. Your choice."

"Patio," she said without thinking. The view was so different from her own, as the barrier island had a different look and feel about it. Plus maybe the breeze and sunshine would keep her alert.

He loaded up plates with bacon and eggs, toast that looked to be a wee bit burnt, and offered her both coffee and juice.

They carried their breakfasts outside and settled beneath the shaded terrace. Connor dug into his food, so she did the same, and one bite reminded her of the fact she hadn't eaten since yesterday... morning?

"So tell me about Rayna," Connor said after

giving her plenty of time to get several bites in. "Besides the fact you like to kayak."

She grimaced at the request and then shrugged. "There's not much to tell. I have two beautiful twin daughters, and I'm a twin myself. That seems to be the thing people find most interesting."

Connor smiled at her, his blue eyes crinkled.

"It's interesting, but I doubt it's the most interesting thing."

"What about you?" she asked, sipping her coffee. "Do I detect a bit of a northern accent?"

"I was born and raised in Texas," he said, feigning a look of horror.

"Really?" she asked, surprised. Working at the decor store, she'd gotten quite good at accents over the years.

"Yup." He leaned toward her, his expression changing over to a handsome grin. "But my mother was from Philly."

"I knew it," she said, her laugh turning into an embarrassing yawn. "Oh, my. Sorry."

"No need for that. You look exhausted."

"It's been a long few days," she said carefully. She pushed her now empty plate away, embarrassed that she'd wolfed it down like a teenaged boy. "I should call my family. I meant to in the guest room but... I'm honestly not sure what to say to them, so I put it off."

Connor's broad hand wrapped around his coffee cup, and he settled back in his chair, his gaze direct and more than a bit unnerving.

"Some might think it obvious why you felt the need to get away."

"Maybe, but... I stole the kayak," she admitted, grimacing. "I've never stolen anything in my life, and yet I just walked up a-and took it off of a kayak rental truck. I'm a *thief*."

Connor's husky chuckles echoed off the stone terrace, and she covered her face with her palms out of embarrassment before shoving her damp hair over her shoulders. "I can't believe I just told you that. You'll be hiding the silver."

"Rayna Jo," he said softly. "People are worried sick about you. They won't care about a *borrowed* kayak. Especially when you return it and pay double for the use of it."

It took her several seconds to realize he knew her name. Her *middle* name.

The air left her lungs in a rush. "You know who I am?"

CHAPTER TEN

Devon snuggled her face deeper into the warmth and velvet-covered hardness and sighed. Why didn't she sleep this well every night?

"Good morning."

She sucked in a gasp at Oz's voice and lifted her head, gasping again when it cracked against his stubbled jawline. "Oh!"

"Ow."

She rubbed her head and watched warily while Oz did the same to his chin. "What time is... We slept out here?"

"Mmm. It appears we did."

Awareness came slowly. She blamed her exhaustion and stressed state for the fact she remained on his lap even after the head-chin collision. "Oh."

She straight-armed her way backwards, but even though she managed to get her butt on the cushion beside him, Oz wrapped a hand around her legs and trapped them.

"Not so fast."

"Oz."

"What?"

She stared at him, wishing she could look half as good as he did in the morning. No doubt her hair was a matted mess and what makeup she hadn't wiped off was now smeared for a fabulously epic raccoon look. "I-I should go check and see if there's been any word."

"There hasn't. Dara was out here a half hour ago."

"She was?"

"You're exhausted. Slept right through it."

Devon groaned softly and rubbed her gritty eyes. There would be a sisterly inquisition in her future. And she didn't have any answers. "How is that possible? Surely someone's seen Mama? It's all over the news and radio, the papers—adding more fuel to the fire of Dad's death *and* the lawsuit. Why hasn't anyone called?"

She'd gone from sleeping to stressed in less than six seconds flat, but she couldn't help it.

Devon felt Oz's hand contract on her leg in a gentle squeeze.

"We'll find her."

But when? And even then—

Her stomach clenched to the point of wanting to hurl.

Even if her mom showed up right this second, would she feel comfortable returning to New York knowing she couldn't return anytime soon? "I'm a horrible person."

Oz blinked at the change in topic.

"Come again?"

She shoved her hands into her hair and clenched her fingers. "I *am*. I'm a horrible person. A horrible daughter."

"How so?"

"Because I'm angry and upset and *ticked off* that I'm going to have to give up the job when all I should care about is my mom," she muttered.

"You've always taken your job seriously. Now you're stressed and torn between family and responsibilities," he said. "It's understandable, Devon."

"Is it?"

"Yes."

"I'm supposed to be back in New York tonight, and considering it takes a minimum of two commercial flights to get there, I need to leave now to make it happen. Instead, I'm going to have to call the network and... How could she just take off like that?"

"Your mom has been through a lot."

"I know. I *know*, but we've all been through a lot," she said, struggling to find her sympathy in light of it screwing up her career. Hadn't they all suffered from her father's behavior? Why was her mother adding to the list?

"I'm sure the network will understand. Give you a few extra days."

Was it possible?

Oz's comment instilled hope but she had her doubts. On that side of the camera, it was dog-eat-dog, and if she couldn't do what needed done, someone else would gladly step into her uncomfortable shoes.

But what else could she do?

Ted wasn't right. Was he? At what point did she start protecting herself from the fallout? Could she even do it? Did she *want to* when it meant distancing herself from the mother who loved her and raised her?

Devon heard the house phone ring and swung

her legs to the porch floor. Two seconds later, she was inside, praying it was good news, only to see Dara wave her closer and hold out the phone.

"It's for you. Someone named Tia?"

Devon pressed a hand to her rolling stomach. It's like the powers that be at the network had heard her mental battle.

She sucked in a fortifying breath and took the portable phone from Dara. "Tia? Hi, what's up?"

"Oh, Devon, thank God," Tia said with her typical drama. "I've called your cell all night and had to convince HR it was an emergency to get them to call you at this number."

"I'm sorry. I'm exhausted and must have slept through the calls. What's going on?" she asked, even though she knew.

"Um, well, they want to know if you're coming back. Like, *now*. Mr. Probst saw the news and was at my desk waiting for me when I got in."

Devon pressed her finger and thumb to the bridge of her nose and squeezed. "Is he there now?"

"No, but I can patch you through to his office."

She needed to caffeinate before this phone call, but since it wasn't possible... "Yeah, do that. Thanks, Tia."

Silence followed her request and then Devon heard Tia clear her throat.

"Are you... coming back? I'm asking because my internship is with you and—"

"Tia, put me through please."

Tia stopped talking, and a second later, the phone clicked. The live network audio sounded in Devon's ear for several moments until the phone clicked again and the chatter stopped.

Devon grimaced when Probst answered the phone with a few choice words, demanding to know where she was. "I'm still in North Carolina. My mother is missing."

"I'm aware of that, but it doesn't change our contract or the job you were hired to do."

"I realize that but... *my mother is missing*. She's not handling things well and... I-I can't come back to New York right now."

"Are you saying what I think you're saying?"

No. No, no, for the love of God, no! "I'm sorry, Mr. Probst. You must see that this scenario isn't exactly normal? Couldn't Simone stay on a few more days? A week? It might give me the time to settle things here."

"I'd like to humor your request, Devon, but that's not possible. Ms. Valentino went into labor this morning and can't even finish her last day. I have to find an anchor in... thirty minutes."

"Mr. Probst—"

"This won't work, Devon. Good luck with your next position. I... hope you find your mother safe and sound."

"Wait, please, I—" The phone clicked in her ear, and she stood there, praying for someone to say it was all a bad joke. A bad dream. Any minute now, she'd wake up and—

"Dev?" Dara asked.

Devon pressed the button on the portable phone to turn it off and quietly set it on the nearby counter above the wine cooler. Even if she drank every bottle, it wouldn't be enough. "Looks like I've been fired."

"Oh, Dev."

Dara rushed toward her and wrapped her in her arms, but after a moment's embrace, Devon pushed her away. "I need a shower."

"Devon?"

Oz. How could she have forgotten about Oz after last night—and this morning?

She shook her head, unable to even look at him because he'd always been able to see through her.

See whatever it was she tried to hide. And right

now, she had to hide the fact she was angry. With her father. Her mother.

Ted.

Life.

Everything.

She hadn't done anything wrong, so why was she on the receiving end of the fallout?

Where was her mother?

Her boyfriend or fiancé or whatever he was?

Why was this happening?

She took off for the stairs without a word and jogged up them, rushing down the hallway toward the bedroom she'd left ten years ago.

She shut the door and leaned against it, refusing to give in to the tears that prickled her eyes.

She was a strong, capable, independent woman. She'd figure it out. She had some savings. Enough to get by for now. It wouldn't last long at New York prices and rental rates, so the race was on, but she could do this. Would do this.

All she had to do was find her mother, find a job... and find out what came next?

OZ STARED at Dara once Devon was out of sight, but other than an expression of concern, Dara didn't speak.

Devon's sister turned on her heel and headed toward the refrigerator, yanking the door open so hard it caused everything inside to rattle.

"She'll find another job," he said, closing the distance between them.

"That's not the problem."

Oz leaned a shoulder against the doorframe and stared at the woman so physically like Devon yet so very different. "It is a lot to take in at once. Devon just needs some space."

"I hope that's all she needs. We definitely don't need Mama and Devon both losing it," Dara said, pouring herself some juice. "Maybe the Babes have some wisdom to impart that'll help."

As though summoned by her statement, the front door opened with a short, quick knock, and Tessa called out a hello.

"Kitchen," Dara said.

Oz turned to see Tessa, Cheryl, and Mary Elizabeth enter, each carrying more dishes of food.

"You love it and you know it," Tessa said, catching his expression.

"You don't hear me complaining," he said,

winking at the women. "Where's Ms. Addy?" he asked.

"Adaline needed to check in at the store," Cheryl said. "I so wish she'd let one of us help her. She insists she can handle things with what help they have, but she's working on some big project, and I can tell it's stressing her."

"Any news about Rayna Jo?" Mary Elizabeth asked.

Dara shook her head but then relayed the result of Devon's conversation.

"Oh, dear."

"Poor girl."

"Does that mean she'll be staying? Moving back?" Mary Elizabeth asked, her tone hopeful. "I know your mother would so love to have both you girls home again. Especially now."

Logan jogged down the stairs and entered the kitchen, looking freshly showered but dressed in the same dark slacks and dress shirt he'd worn yesterday for the funeral.

"Hey, how's every— What happened? Has there been news?" he asked.

Dara gave him the rundown of the moment, and Oz watched as Logan glanced at him once the ladies went back to chatting. Oz braced himself when Logan meandered his way.

"You must be happy about this turn of events," Logan said in a low voice.

"She's entangled," Oz said, using Devon's description of her relationship.

"It's only a matter of time before she sees the guy is a jerk."

"I'm not so sure about that. She obviously likes something about him. You know what? It doesn't matter. I just want her to be happy."

"Because that's how love's supposed to be. Do you not believe that's possible here—with you?"

"It wasn't before." Oz shrugged. "Why would that change now?"

———

HIS STATEMENT to Logan stayed with Oz long after the conversation had ended. He ran home long enough to shower and change, thinking how great it would be if only Devon's things were in the closet beside his.

Once he'd dressed again, he shoveled down a quick sandwich and headed back to the Teekses' to begin searching again.

He prayed Rayna Jo stayed strong and didn't let fear make any decisions for her. Losing one parent was bad enough. Losing two in the same week?

Carrying a bottle of water with him, he locked up and left the house, taking the boardwalk on the off chance Rayna Jo might make an appearance.

When he arrived at the Teekses', he let himself in after a quick knock, well able to remember all the times he'd arrived on the porch for a day in the sun with Devon before their dating years had even begun. "Any news?" he asked once he made his way to the kitchen.

Dara and Devon shook their heads simultaneously and his thoughts grew grim. "I thought I'd head out again to look."

"I'll go with you," Devon said. "I can't stand sitting here doing nothing."

"I'll stay," Dara said. "In case she comes back."

Without speaking, he and Devon made their way through the house to the door. "Have you talked to your...Ted?"

The words emerged out of nowhere, and he winced at the sound of them. Even he could hear the jealousy loud and clear.

"Today's his luncheon."

"So that's a no?"

"Why does it matter?" Devon stopped on the porch steps to face him. "You and I are just friends, Oz. If you can't accept that, maybe we shouldn't..."

She lifted a hand and waved it in the air like that would explain the tension between them.

"Friends talk about things. Important things."

She turned and descended the rest of the way.

"That may be true, but in our case, I think it's best if we keep things... light."

"Light? Like the weather?"

"You know what I mean."

"I do. I just can't help but think there's another reason you're avoiding the deep topics that are actually important."

He fell into step beside her and gently took her elbow in his hand to steer her right instead of left since he'd just come from that direction.

"I don't want to fight with you."

"Good. I don't want to fight with you either."

"What *do* you want, Oz? And don't say me again."

"There you go, avoiding the truth." He heard her release a frustrated sound, convinced it meant he was getting to her.

"Okay, fine. You want me. But guess what? I'm not available. There. Subject closed."

"You do know you can do better?"

"Do better? He's on track to be the next governor of New York. It's only a matter of time."

"I guess if that matters to you, I never realized how shallow you were."

She stopped in her tracks and faced him, hands fisted.

"First I can do better, then I'm shallow. Which is it? Hmm? Because I think you're deliberately trying to pick a fight because you're frustrated I won't cave to your wishes."

He took a step closer and lowered his head to better see into her eyes.

"I am frustrated, but not for that reason. Has it not occurred to you that he chose his career over you? Over your *missing mother?*"

She swallowed audibly and lowered her lashes, avoiding his gaze.

"Which is what I did to you. I've said I'm sorry, Oz."

"I don't want your apologies. I want to know that if you marry this guy and come second or *fifth* in his life due to his choices, that you'll be okay. I speak from experience when I say it's not fun being left behind."

He straightened and moved away from her,

walking on, but four steps later, she grabbed hold of his forearm and tugged.

"Wait."

"What?"

"I hate this, okay? I hate fighting with you."

"Then don't. Kiss me instead." He lowered his head because at that moment he wanted nothing more than to kiss her as deeply and passionately as he'd dreamed about last night on the swing holding her.

But Devon drew back and held up her hand.

"If you can't handle us remaining friends, maybe we should keep our distance. I'm heading back to the house."

Oz watched her walk away, the sway of her hips and her long braid calling to him like a siren's song.

He raked a hand over his face and growled out his frustration. Unrequited love bit the big one.

———

RAYNA STARTLED when a seagull squawked close by. She lifted her lashes and gasped, shoving herself upright and drawing Connor's attention from where he sat. "I fell asleep."

He lowered the newspaper and folded it neatly,

setting it aside before joining her. "You're exhausted. And confession is good for the soul. You fell asleep the moment you finished telling me your story."

Memories came flooding back, that of Connor admitting he'd seen several news segments about her disappearance and how he'd recognized her on the beach. "What you must think of me."

"I think you're overwhelmed and for good reason. Anyone in your position would be hard-pressed not to be."

Yes, well, reason or not, she had to face the consequences of her actions. "I have to call my family. I have to go back a-and sort this mess out."

He settled himself in a chair to her right, and she found his presence comforting despite having known him a matter of hours. How was that possible?

"You do have to contact your family and let them know you're okay. Whether you go back is up to you. You're welcome to stay a few days. Rest."

Her breath froze in her lungs for a long second before she exhaled. "You don't even know me."

A low chuckle rumbled out of his chest, and she found herself drawn to the sound.

"Yes, well, I know enough. And even though my kids would probably think I'm crazy, I know what it's like to want to disappear."

"You do?"

"After my wife died," he said, nodding, "I struggled. I didn't understand how evil walks the earth but my never-hurt-a-soul wife was taken. Still don't, truth be told. I imagine facing what you face isn't much different."

Rayna hugged her arms around her front. "It's hard to accept that I'll lose everything because of him."

"Then don't. At least not yet. Cases like this are often settled or thrown out. Give it time."

His words washed over her. "I'm... embarrassed. *Mortified*. A bit heartbroken—but not in the way I should be. I'm also angry with myself. That I put up with his behavior for so many years, and now I wonder why. *Why* did I do it?"

"Love's a complicated thing," Connor said.

She nodded. "I did love him. You can't spend that many years with someone and not love. But while my daughters are mourning their father, I'm beyond angry that he's left me in the position I find myself in. I'm angry that he doesn't have to deal with this but I do. Does that make me a bad person?"

Connor sat forward in the chair, his elbows on his knees, hands clasped together in front of him.

"Not at all. And he'll deal with it, one way or

another," Connor said. "Now, this is none of my business, but the newspaper article I just read said you'd had some sort of memory issue recently?"

Rayna released a soft groan. "I have no secrets left, do I?" she said, grimacing. "The stress and circumstances of Richard's death were difficult for me to accept. I was confused for a day or two and thought he was away on business. But I'm okay now."

"Hon, you might remember it now, but kayaking from Carolina Cove to Bald Head Island while wearing your mourning dress... I don't think that'd qualify as being okay."

A laugh burst out of her at the absurdity. "I suppose not. But like I said, I had to get away from all of those looks I was getting. I couldn't pretend to be the mournful wife a moment longer when I boiled with anger inside."

"I imagine not."

"Getting served the lawsuit papers at the cemetery was the icing on the cake," she said, smoothing her hand over the pattern on the sundress. "I'd like to bring Richard back from the dead just so I can strangle him and kill him again. I suppose I have more pride and vanity than I thought."

Connor chuckled and nodded.

"I'd say any wife would feel the same in your shoes."

She closed her burning eyes and opened them again to stare out at the beautiful day. Life moved on, no matter what someone might be going through. "What am I going to do? What if I lose everything because of him?" she asked. "My home, my business?"

"Now, don't let what-ifs get you. You know, I don't believe in coincidences. Do you?"

"Not really. But I'm not following."

"I might be able to help you with your problem, Rayna."

"How so?"

He winked at her. "Once upon a time, I was a darn good attorney. Every now and again, I dust off my diploma and help out a friend. We can talk about that later, though." He reached into his pocket and pulled out a cell phone, holding it out for her. "Call your family. Tell them you're safe. When you're ready, I'll take you home."

She took the phone, hand trembling as she stared at him. "When I'm ready?"

"It's a big house. Someone could be in my guest rooms a week and I wouldn't even know it."

She laughed softly at the thought. "My daughter

is in cybersecurity. If I use your phone, it won't be long before she'll come knocking on your door."

"That's fine, too. Heck, invite your daughters here. I'll fix us up some food and we can talk about your case."

"You're serious," she said. "Why would you do such a thing for someone you don't know?"

She watched as he tilted his head to one side and stared at her with those warm blue eyes of his.

"Us widows and widowers have to stick together." He tapped the arm of the settee where she sat and stood. "Call them," he said again as he walked away. "Tell 'em I've got some good steaks and seafood just begging to be grilled."

Rayna stared at the phone screen for a long moment before swiping to make a call. The only numbers she knew by heart were her own and the house phone, so she tried the home phone first. It rang once. Twice.

"Hello?"

Rayna squeezed her eyes shut and inhaled. "Mary Elizabeth, is that you?"

"*Rayna Jo,*" her friend cried, happiness apparent in her tone. "Where *are* you?"

There was a lot of commotion in the background, and it was all too easy to imagine the Babes and her daughters scrambling toward Mary Elizabeth to listen in. "I'm safe. I'm sorry for scaring everyone."

"Where?" Mary Elizabeth asked again.

"Mama, it's Devon. Tell us where you are so we can come get you."

"Whose phone is this? I don't recognize the number," Dara said.

"I'm... I'm on Bald Head Island."

"What are you doing out there?" Mary Elizabeth asked.

"How did you *get* there?" Devon asked.

"None of that matters. Just give us an address and we'll come get you," Cheryl said.

Feeling pressured by all of the questions even though their concern was evident, Rayna shook her head. "Um, I'm not sure—"

"Mama, who is Connor Sennett?" Dara asked, voice lifted.

Well, that hadn't taken long. "He's a friend."

"A friend? Mama, are you... Is he..." Devon tried to ask.

Realizing how it must have sounded, Rayna sighed. "No, I am not having an affair," she stated dryly. "I met Connor this morning. He's letting me use his phone."

"So where are you now?" Dara asked. "Are you at a hotel?"

"N-no. I'm at his home."

"Mama, that doesn't sound like you," Devon said. "Tell us his address. Let us come get you."

"He said he could bring me home. Or y-you girls could come here."

"I've got the address," Dara said.

Her talented daughter never failed to amaze. "Good. While you make your way here, I'm going to go rest."

"Mama," Devon said, "are you sure you're safe?"

Rayna pondered the many implications of that question and nodded. "Yes, sweetheart. I am. I'll see you soon?"

CHAPTER ELEVEN

The moment Dara tracked the address of Connor Sennett, everyone wanted to rush to Bald Head Island to retrieve Rayna Jo.

Thankfully, Logan convinced the Babes that a select few should go in order to not pressure her mother into another disappearing act.

So Devon, Dara, Logan, and Adaline now sat shoulder to shoulder on the ferry taking them to Bald Head Island, all of them lost in their own thoughts during the twenty-minute ride from Southport after a forty-minute ferry from Ft. Fisher. Thankfully they'd arrived just as the ferry was loading and managed to get onboard right away.

Devon stared out at the water, once again

reminded of how much she'd actually missed this area. Oh, she could go to the Hamptons to the beach or ride a ferry around Staten Island, but it wasn't the same. It wasn't this.

The beauty of the south, the sandbars and islands, grasses and shorelines, called to her with the comfort of a child's lullaby. She knew these sounds, smells, sights—like nothing else.

The drone of the ferry's engine filled her ears, and she glanced around, noting the passengers ranged in age from young to old and included every social background.

She saw workers with steel-toed boots and coolers holding their lunches. Parents obviously vacationing with luggage and children, as well as some older couples, their lack of bags a good indicator that they lived on the island. There were also a variety of singles, some with golf clubs, some wearing name tags and dressed as though they were about to start a work shift.

Bet we're the only ones going to retrieve a sixty-three-year-old runaway, she mused.

The ferry sounded the alert they as neared their destination, and Devon tried to brace herself for what she might find when they tracked her mother down.

Had Mama lied? Was she *also* having an affair? Who was this Connor person?

They departed the ferry and quickly made their way to the golf cart rental. There were very few vehicles on the island, and those were usually construction and emergency vehicles. Those who lived here kept vehicles parked at the marina in Southport. As a whole, the island used golf carts or bikes to get around.

"Got it. Let's go," Logan said, having secured a golf cart for six.

They piled in with Adaline sitting in the passenger seat beside her son. Devon felt Dara watching her and knew her time was up.

"Are you ever going to say anything?" Dara asked, voice low so as to not be heard by those in front of them.

"What do you want me to say? It wasn't planned."

"You slept with him."

"I did not, not the way *that* sounds. I literally slept because I was exhausted and wrecked after everything that happened."

"You must not be too wrecked," Dara said. "Which makes me wonder—how do you go from sending your boyfriend off to New York to *sleeping on Oz?*"

She brushed her hair away from her face, but it blew right back again. "I'm not sure."

"You know he's still hung up on you."

"We're just friends."

"Dev, seriously?"

"I *know*, okay?" she said, acknowledging her comment. "He told me, but nothing's changed."

"*Every*thing's changed. Without a job you have no reason to go rushing back to New York now—"

"That doesn't mean I want to stay in Carolina Cove. And what about Ted?"

"What about him? You marry that guy and you're asking for a lifetime of trouble."

"You don't even know him."

"I know enough. Besides, for someone who showed up a week ago looking sick from stress, a week here has you looking better *despite* the horrific circumstances. Doesn't that tell you something?"

"Yeah, I need to tan more," she said, refusing to throw in the towel.

Dara muttered something Devon couldn't make out, but her sister's expression made the sentiment clear.

"How do you not see that Ted's a jerk? I can't believe you'd even consider marrying that guy."

"He *had* to leave. He has important responsibilities to uphold."

"His first one should've been to you. He should be here now."

"You sound like Oz," Devon muttered.

"Good. Because he's right. He's been here for you this whole time. Tell me you see that."

"Oz is a good *friend*," she stressed.

"I know you still have feelings for him, too."

She did. She always would.

But now?

Ten years later?

She knew what Oz expected of her. But she wasn't ready to give up on her dream. Or New York.

But wouldn't that happen once she and Ted were married? What if he did manage to become governor down the line? Wouldn't she have to give it all up then? Oz was right, Ted's career would come first. Be a priority for both of them and hers would take a nosedive no matter what.

"Just don't hurt him, Dev. Not again. You weren't here so you didn't see Oz last time. You don't know how bad it was. Michael was really worried about him. We all were."

If it was anything like she'd felt, she knew all too well how bad Oz had been. But she'd had her new job and the excitement of the move to focus on and keep her going. What had Oz focused on? "That's the last thing I'd want."

"Then get it together," Dara said. "Sleeping in his arms? You don't think that's sending signals you shouldn't be sending?"

Devon didn't answer. Couldn't. Because she knew Dara was right. Oz had snuggled her close last night to comfort her, but she should've shoved him away. Kept a boundary.

She walked a tightrope where Oz was concerned. Because it would be so easy to allow herself to lean on him even more than she already had. Allow him to comfort her because she so desperately needed it.

To... kiss her?

What would Dara say if she knew about the kiss on the beach?

As Logan pushed the golf cart to its maximum speed down the paved paths toward one end of the island, Devon watched the scenery fly by.

Beautiful pines and live oaks, palm trees, crepe myrtles. Such a difference from concrete buildings and skyscrapers.

Sometimes she got tired of the noise and the traffic and the unpleasant aromas that made the city what it was. She missed her family and friends so badly, and a phone call wouldn't do, but—

"There. That's it," Adaline said.

She and Dara both looked to see where their aunt pointed. Devon couldn't stop the small gasp that escaped when she took in the massive beautiful home up ahead.

Logan wheeled the cart into a particular driveway, and everyone raced toward the door. On the porch, however, they all looked at each other before Logan finally stretched out a long, tanned arm and rang the doorbell.

Dara tapped her foot impatiently, and Devon gripped her fingers so tight they went numb. Finally they heard footsteps on the other side of the door before a man opened it and did a double take. "Well now, it doesn't take much to know who you are," he said, his attention on Adaline. From there his gaze shifted to Devon and Dara and he smiled.

"Mr....Sennett?" Logan said.

"Call me Connor," he said. "You're Adaline," he said, greeting her aunt.

"Yes. This is my son, Logan, and my nieces—"

"Wait, let me guess," Connor said, shaking hands

with Logan before the man's attention shifted back to them. After a second of pondering, he waggled a finger in the air toward Dara.

"Dara, right? Which makes you Devon?"

They both nodded and shook hands with him.

"Your mother described you perfectly. Though I probably wouldn't have guessed correctly had you not been wearing boots at the beach," he said to Dara, amusement lighting his eyes.

Dara had always had a distinctive style. Combat boots paired with camo shorts and a black skull and crossbones T-shirt completed today's ensemble, whereas Devon wore a knee-length gray romper over a sleeveless dove-gray blouse and low sandals.

"Come on inside," Connor said, stepping back and swinging the door wide.

Dara glanced at Devon before stepping forward and leading the charge.

"Where's our mother?"

"Rayna's resting in one of the guest rooms. I don't think she slept all night, so maybe you shouldn't wake her just yet. I was just fixing some lunch. I hope you'll join me?"

The four of them exchanged glances before following the man through the large entry, past several rooms, and on into the kitchen.

"How did you meet our mother?" Dara asked the man.

He nodded and waved toward the wall of windows. Devon noted he liked to talk with his hands.

"Saw her down on the beach this morning. I'd heard the report about a missing woman but certainly didn't expect to stumble upon her."

"So you didn't know each other before this morning?" Devon asked, trying to keep the suspicion from her voice but having a hard time.

"No. Rayna told me about your daddy's death. I'm sorry about that," he said. "Awful thing to have to go through on top of everything else."

"Thank you," Dara and Devon said in unison.

"Have a seat," he said, extending an arm toward the living area. "Can I get anyone a drink? I've got cold water, sodas, some juices. Heavier stuff if it's not too early for you."

It seemed odd to be standing in a stranger's house politely chatting about her mother, and Devon looked at Logan for backup. "You should go check on her."

Logan glanced at the man and Devon watched the exchange.

"I'm a doctor," Logan said to Connor. "If you

don't mind, I would like to see my aunt. I'll do my best not to wake her."

The man lifted his hand and pointed toward an open area in the distance.

"Of course. Straight through there. First door on the left. I heard some noise after she went inside though, like she blocked the door with a chair."

"And that didn't concern you?" Devon asked.

"A woman alone in a stranger's house? Not really. She did it earlier and came out when she was ready."

Logan headed toward the guest room while Devon paced to the windows. "That's quite the view."

"It is. Now, who wants steaks and who wants chicken?"

Devon heard Logan returning and saw him shrug.

"Door's locked."

"Do you have a key?" Devon asked Connor. "She hasn't been well. I think it's important we check on her."

"I do. And I understand your thinking, but the woman I met was calm and clear-headed. I don't think she's a danger to anyone or herself."

"And you know this after an hour or two with her?" Dara asked.

Connor smiled and moved toward a pantry. Inside he stared at the wall until selecting a key, holding it out to Logan.

"I've seen a lot of crazy over the years, hon. Your mama ain't it."

Logan took the key but then snapped his fingers and pointed at the man.

"Connor Sennett... I *knew* I recognized the name. You're the writer Oz meets up with every now and again to talk publishing."

"You're an author?" Devon asked, glancing between the two men.

Connor looked surprised by their connection to Oz but nodded.

"Attorney, author, and beach bum," the man said.

"He writes legal thrillers," Logan added. "Oz is my brother's best friend," he said to Connor, filling in the missing piece.

"Now that is a small world connection," Connor murmured, nodding. "But not too uncommon in this area. Islands are only so big."

"That's why you said you've seen crazy? You meant in court?" Dara asked.

Connor nodded. "Girls, your mama is reeling and exhausted but calm and clear. Whatever happened to her before... she's pulled herself through to the other side. Doesn't mean she won't have dark days ahead, but I think she's found her strength."

"Really?" Devon asked, struggling to believe the statement.

Connor smiled yet again, and she found herself warming up to the man. Even if it was because he gave her some hope.

"Really. Now, which would you like on your salad, young lady? I haven't seen Oscar in a couple of months. Should we call him up and tell him to hop a ferry on over here?"

RAYNA JO HEARD a noise and bolted upright on the bed. The bedroom door opened but the chair under the knob didn't allow it to open far.

A familiar low mutter sounded, and she shoved herself up and off the comfortable mattress, peeking through the inch or so crack in the door until she spotted her nephew on the other side.

"I didn't mean to wake you," he said apologetically. "Can I, uh, come in?"

Rayna bent and pulled the chair away and the door swung open. She'd barely had time to straighten before Logan pulled her against his chest for a hug.

"You scared us, Ray-Ray."

She felt bad for that and hugged her nephew with all the love she'd felt from the moment he and his brother were born. "I'm sorry. I just couldn't breathe after what happened at the cemetery. I had to get away."

He let go of her and gently nudged her back toward the bed, his hand sliding down her arm to take her pulse.

"I'm fine, Logan. Better than I've been since all of this began. It's amazing what a nighttime adventure will do to force someone to find their courage."

"How did you get here?" he asked.

"I stole a kayak." She laughed when she saw his expression turn to shock. "I know. So unlike me. I hope I don't get in too much trouble for it, but I don't regret it. And of course I'll return it and pay for its use."

"Rayna J—"

"Don't give me that tone," she ordered.

"If he can't, I will," Adaline said from the doorway.

Her twin rushed inside and across the bedroom,

hugging Rayna with such force she nearly toppled them both.

"Don't you *ever* do something like that again. You scared the dickens out of me."

Rayna returned the hug and released her sister, breathing in the soft scent of her perfume. "I make no promises. It was exactly what I needed, and if I need to do it again, I will," she stated determinedly.

"Ray-Ray, do you remember what happened? Do you have any foggy areas?"

"I remember it all. I'm fine, Logan. Truly. Just tired and... resigned."

He studied her for a long moment as though assessing her words and demeanor before he nodded.

"I'll let you two talk," Logan said, straightening from his crouched position in front of her to kiss her cheek and take his leave.

The door shut softly behind Logan, and Rayna prepared herself for the lecture she knew she'd receive.

"I thought you'd hurt yourself," Adaline said, voice tight. "That you'd *left* me."

"I thought about it. I thought about a lot of things," she said, admitting the darkness had almost won, "but then... I got angry. Why should I allow Richard's idiocy to ruin my life? If it happens and I lose everything, then I suppose it's God's will. Isn't that what Mother would tell us?"

"She'd say, *Earthly possessions aren't ever ours. Love them too much and watch how quickly they'll get taken away.*"

Adaline patted Rayna's hand and squeezed it tightly.

"We'll find a way to fix this. It'll all be fine," her sister said.

"I hope so. But if the worst does happen? I realize after last night, that's okay, too."

Adaline's eyes widened like she knew Rayna meant what she said.

"Rayna Jo—"

"Rayna," she corrected gently, feeling a bit silly over the name thing but determined to stand her ground. "Rayna Jo was weak. Rayna isn't," she said, holding Adaline's gaze. "I'm *not* Rayna Jo anymore. I won't be disrespected or cower from problems. I won't. Whatever happens, Rayna will be okay."

Adaline lifted her hand and smoothed Rayna's hair over her shoulder.

"That must have been some come-to-Jesus journey last night."

"It was."

"You know, you'll be pleased to hear all of this has opened my eyes to some things as well."

"Oh?" Rayna asked.

"You were right about Dale. That night I went to his condo, he tried to do more than flirt. Tried *hard*," Adaline said, giving her a look.

"And?" Rayna asked, searching her sister's face.

"And... I was tempted, I admit. Then we got the news about Richard and... thankfully, it opened my eyes and I got out of there."

"Oh, Adaline."

"No, it's good. It was the best thing that happened. This mess with Richard has made me rethink things. I can't believe I'd even consider ruining my marriage. I don't know what I was thinking. I'm so glad Dara contacted me before anything happened."

"Me, too."

"I'd never want to hurt Hugh the way Richard hurt you, and through all of this, Hugh has been a saint," she said. "I took it for granted. All of it."

"I think a lot of people do after a while."

"I'm ashamed of it. Hugh has always been around whenever I needed him and is such a good man. Richard wasn't around that often for you, and you still mourn him."

"You lost focus for a moment, but you won't allow yourself to do that again. I'm glad you see things clearly now," Rayna said.

"Me, too. Though I hate that it came as a result of all that's happened to you. Oh—once things calm down? I'm thinking of surprising Hugh with a second honeymoon. He's *always* wanted to go to Alaska, and I've put him off. I think it's time we go."

A knock sounded on the door and Rayna called out to come in. The door opened and her girls appeared.

"Mama? Are you okay?" Devon asked, watching Rayna with a wary expression.

Rayna stood and opened her arms, and Devon and Dara rushed to hug her. "I'm fine. I'm better than fine now that you're here. I'm sorry I scared you," she said before kissing both their cheeks. "I just needed time to myself."

"Mama, we'll figure something out with the lawsuit," Dara said. "Adam's going through the legal stuff now. It'll be all right."

She hugged her girls again. So long as she had them, she'd be fine. "I know."

"Mr.— Connor made lunch. Are you hungry?" Devon asked. "I think he'd like to feed us before we head back to the ferry."

Rayna smiled and ran a hand over Dara's long braid. "Starving," she said, realizing that her appetite had already returned.

"Did you know Connor knows Oz?"

Rayna smiled. "Actually, that doesn't surprise me at all. Not much can at this point."

———

OZ STARED down at the empty computer screen in front of him, the blinking cursor mocking his attempts to meet his deadline. He had a book due to his editor by the end of the month, and now that Rayna Jo had been found, he'd locked himself inside his office to get some pages written. Not writing since Devon's arrival had definitely put him behind.

As did coming up with a plausible escape for his heroine.

You've done it before; you can do it again. How many books have you written?

Feeling like a hack and an imposter was normal for any writer, but there came a time when he had to set aside the distractions, the doubts, and concerns that this book would be the last due to it being a disaster and push through.

Now was one of those—

His cell phone buzzed, and he muttered when he knocked over a mostly empty glass of water while retrieving it.

He used a napkin leftover from who knows when to sop up the water splashed over his notes while staring at the phone screen.

We have Rayna. She's fine. Heading back soon.

The mass text from Devon was sent to everyone in their group, and he found himself clicking off of it and onto Devon's name. *How are you?* he typed.

He saw the three dots appear indicating she wrote a reply, but then they disappeared, and seconds passed with no text.

Finally the dots appeared again and then—

We need to talk.

"Four terrifying words every man dreads hearing," he muttered to himself. To her, he wrote, *Dinner. Pick you up at seven.*

This is exactly what we need to talk about. This isn't a date.

A low chuckle emerged at her response, and he sighed, thumbs flying. *Whatever you say.*

Maybe she'd be happy with that answer. He, on the other hand, would take his chances and hope her agreement was—to use her words—a toe in the door and a step in the right direction. Maybe he was crazy to open himself up to heartbreak again, but something inside of him urged him to give it one last shot. She wasn't married yet. *BTW how did Rayna get to BHI?*

She stole a kayak! Left Ft. Fisher and cruised all the way to Bald Head Island. See you @ seven.

A shocked laugh emerged from him at the news, and he tossed the phone aside to focus on his computer. The cursor blinked insidiously, but a thought formed and then...

The scene began to form in his head, and his fingers flew across the old-fashioned typewriter-style keyboard his father had gifted him at Christmas.

His determined heroine ran as fast as she could. She ignored the briars and sharp limbs slicing into her legs, hiding behind trees and bushes and rocks as she fled her captor.

She saw an old shed up ahead. A place to hide? Find a weapon?

She glanced over her shoulder, her imagination running rampant because it turned shadows into the monster of a man who'd kidnapped her hours before.

The shed was dark and dank, and she held in a scream as something scampered across her foot, brushed against her lower leg as it fled out the door she'd left open.

Other than a stack of old buckets and a few bales of moldy hay seen by the light of the moon shining in through the hole in the roof, the shed appeared empty. There were no pitchforks or shovels or anything that would help.

Desperate, she rounded the shed and tripped over something in the dark, falling face-first into the wet, mossy sand. Her ankle throbbed, but when she turned her head—

An old kayak leaned up against the outside of the building. Who knew if it leaked, but there was only one way to find out.

Limping, gasping, she grabbed the paddle she'd tripped over and tossed it in, then dragged the kayak into the murky depths of the nearby stream.

She paddled away, the current aiding her, just as her kidnapper broke through the scrub behind her and roared in rage.

HOURS LATER, Oz still typed, the words flowing like they hadn't for quite some time. He'd always been a plotter, but he also wrote by the seat of his pants in how he got from plot point to plot point.

With his heroine on the run and getting sucked

farther and farther downstream, her kidnapper was in hot pursuit. But he wasn't the only danger she faced as she paddled through the murky trenches of the marshes.

Oz typed until his arms ached and he ran out of words, finishing the scene in a place that would help him get started tomorrow and whistling at the word count he'd racked up.

In a matter of hours, he'd made up for the time he'd lost during the week. Keep up the pace and he'd have no problem hitting his deadline. He just had to figure out what came next.

He glanced at the clock on the wall and shoved his chair away from the desk. Thanks to his push to get his words down, he now had to rush to shower and get ready for his dinner with Devon.

Thankfully it didn't take long, and he was on his way to Rayna's house in no time.

"You're late," Devon said as he made his way up the walk.

He turned his head, spotting her in the swing hanging from the gnarled live oak on the corner of their property. "I'm right on time," he countered, changing direction. "How's Rayna?"

"Exhausted. She's already in bed."

"She stole a kayak?" he asked. "I have to hear that story."

He watched as Devon grimaced, her hands gripping the seat of the swing a little tighter.

"I can't stand thinking about it, to be honest. The current, snakes, *alligators*. When I think of what could've happened to her..."

"But it didn't. She's fine," he said, hoping the reminder would bring comfort.

One of the things he'd learned over the years was that everything was fodder for story. Small details became big ones at just the right time. "Logan said in the group text her mind seems clear?"

"Crystal. She's calm, too. Like, ridiculously so. It's like she found some magic potion on the water."

"Maybe she did. Sometimes it takes facing the scariest challenges in life to make us realize our strength. Maybe last night was her realization."

He shoved his hands into the pockets of his shorts, taking in her appearance as she remained on the swing.

She wore green shorts and a white top, nothing fancy, but she looked beautiful. No wonder the camera loved her. "How about we continue this discussion on the way to the restaurant? I booked us a table at Eddie's."

"Oz, this isn't a date."

"You still have to eat. And so do I. I've been writing all day and haven't eaten since breakfast." He tilted his head. "Mushroom ravioli," he coaxed, naming her favorite dish from memory. "Come on. As much as I love the Babes' cooking, you have to be getting tired of heating up leftovers, yeah?"

———

WITH ONE LAST wary look at Oz's handsome face, Devon stood and fell into step beside him. Oz would have to remember her favorite meal and coerce her with it. The memory alone left her mouth watering.

Eddie's was located near the pier, which meant they could easily walk. They meandered across the road to the boardwalk, elbows brushing periodically. Seagulls squawked overhead and grackles made that weird little chirp they made, the blue-green sheen in their shiny black feathers brilliant as they perused them from their high perch atop signs listing the rules for the beach.

"Dara lectured me on the way to get Mama," Devon said, figuring maybe it was best to talk first and then... maybe dinner would happen, maybe it wouldn't.

"About?"

"You."

"Do I want to know what she said?"

She peeked up at him, trying to gauge his reaction as she said, "She warned me not to hurt you again."

"I see. Well, I'm a big boy, Dev."

"I know but... I get the feeling if I cooperated you'd... maybe like to pick right back up where we left off."

"Would that be a bad thing?"

She took two more steps and then stopped, turning to face him and thankful this end of the long boardwalk remained quiet even during the tourist season. There were a few people hanging out on nearby porches but no one within hearing distance. "Yes. I'm involved to someone else."

His gaze narrowed on her and she saw anger flare a bit in his tight expression.

"Believe me, I'm aware. The reason that doesn't bother me quite as much as it should is because I don't believe you're happy. You just haven't admitted it to yourself yet."

Not happy? She had a wonderful life. A

wonderful job—well, *had*, but... Ted was a good man. A solid man. If you didn't hold not being a priority against him. "My happi— my life is none of your concern."

"I disagree. Look, I only want the best for you, Devon. That includes love. Real love."

"I have that."

Oz didn't say a word. He didn't have to. He merely lifted one thick eyebrow high and stared at her to the point she wanted to stomp her feet. Okay, so her relationship with Ted wasn't something from a romance novel, but happiness was... relative.

Right? "Look," she said, her impatience flooding her tone. "We couldn't make it work ten years ago, and ten years later, nothing's changed."

"I disagree."

"How so?"

"Your job, for starters."

She lifted her chin. "I'll find another one."

"I'm sure you will, but why bother?"

A gasp left her. "What do you mean?"

"Come on, Dev. Future governor's wives make for pretty pictures and charity speeches. They don't work an outside job, especially not one as public as yours would be."

Ted was all for her working right now, but her

position at a network could positively influence a campaign. Would that change as he climbed the political tiers?

What do you think? "We'll discuss it when we reach that crossroads," she said tightly.

"There won't be a discussion and you know it. You'll work until then and give up your dream to show your support for him."

Oz echoed her thoughts and worries, those she'd barely acknowledged herself because of what they meant. Was she that woman? Her... *mother?* "Oz, I think we should... I don't want to hurt you."

"Then don't."

"You're making it difficult," she said, the words emerging tight.

"Good. If it was easy, I wouldn't be trying hard enough to get you to see your future."

"Fine. But even if something happens and I don't marry Ted, that doesn't mean I'm meant to be with you. Oz... Mama already told you that you're broken glass. Is that what you want to be?"

He drew back, his head lifting, turning, to stare out at the ocean for a long moment before shifting his attention back to her, a wry smile curling his lips. "Maybe I am because of what happened with us before, but after ten years, what if I'm that rare piece just waiting to be rediscovered?"

A low huff left her. Leave it to the writer to come up with that kind of comparison. But Oz definitely qualified as rare, and she'd be lying if she denied that.

He was the man any girl would be lucky to take home to their mother. A man who could be trusted alone with her girlfriends. Oz wasn't a player, never had been, and she knew in her soul he'd ruined her in a lot of ways because no one else would ever measure up to him.

Not even Ted, with his handsome good looks, drive to succeed, and aspirations.

She loved Ted, but he used his handsome face to win over female voters. Flirting, complimenting, admiring.

Now aware of her father's behavior, she remembered his flirtatious attitude and statements and couldn't help but wonder...

Was she setting herself up for the same heartbreak as her mother?

Really? Was she going to go down that path?

It's familiar, her mind said.

"Controllable," she whispered.

"What was that?" Oz asked her. "I can hear the cranks turning in that brain of yours."

She blinked to awareness and tried to master a

neutral expression, uneasy with her revelation. "You're wrong," she said, determined to go down swinging.

"You know you can't lie to me."

Hands fisted, she moved toward a bench and sat with her back to the road and the homes behind them. Oz followed but chose to sit on the railing, facing her.

"You want a confession? Fine. You weren't the only one heartbroken when we ended. That decision... it wasn't easy for me."

"Good. That means I wasn't the only one actually in love."

She glanced up at him and found him leaning toward her, hands gripping the wooden railing by his hips. "You weren't, Oz. But I think a part of me... knew."

"Knew what?"

Was she really going to confess this? "Knew that if I stayed, I'd always wonder what if? I'd wind up resenting you and us and... everything."

"You weren't ready."

She nodded and stood, taking a few steps to get them moving again so she wouldn't have a hundred fifty percent of Oz's undivided attention while she waded through the muck that was life. "I've wanted to be on air and have my own show for as long as I can remember. I *played* TV news anchor as a kid. I have no idea why, but it's all I've ever—" She broke off, unable to continue because her thoughts shifted to the future. To Ted. After a couple of steps, she turned and tried again. "I do think about what'll happen when I marry Ted."

"And?"

It's what made her want to reevaluate. Made her realize what she'd first thought was a fairy tale was in fact a Kennedy-esque romance complete with an unhappy ending. One she wasn't sure she could live.

"Look, Devon, I know I have no right to comment on your life, but I hope you'll thoroughly think this through. At least think of alternative ways to keep doing something you obviously love."

"You make it sound easy," she said.

"No. But I do think it's doable."

"I think my father is the perfect example that you can't have your cake and eat it, too," she stated dryly.

"If it's important, if it really means something to you, Devon, it's worth fighting for. Why do you think I'm still trying?"

CHAPTER TWELVE

They didn't go to dinner.

After Oz's comment, Devon decided she was too tired to eat and insisted on walking home—alone.

Now Oz sat at the bar inside of Eddie's, the plate in front of him mostly untouched.

"Tell me it's not happening again," Michael said from behind before clamping a hand down on Oz's shoulder. "You look like you'd crawl into that drink if you could."

Oz huffed and twisted his head to see Michael taking the stool beside him. Eddie's was a small mom-and-pop restaurant with the best Italian food for miles. The key word, however, was small, and the noise level of the many families squeezed into booths and around tables was giving Oz a headache. Or maybe it was the fact he'd never stopped loving a woman he apparently couldn't have. "I'm fine."

"Keep repeating it and maybe it'll be true," his buddy said. "So rumor has it you left this evening with a certain gorgeous woman but then she was seen returning home alone soon after. Did you have a fight?"

Sometimes living in a fishbowl sucked. This was one of those times. "Dara lectured Dev and warned her off of hurting me again."

"And you told her it was impossible because you never actually got over her in the first place?"

"Is there a reason you're spoiling my dinner?" Oz asked.

The bartender stopped by and asked if she could get Michael anything, and he placed an order for a drink.

"So you're staying," Oz mused, thinking he ought to ask for a box and take his food to go.

"Can't leave my best friend sitting alone looking like his dog died. So what'd Dev say when you talked to her?"

"You really want to sit here and gossip like teenage girls?" Oz asked.

"You got anything better to do?"

He should be writing. Researching. Cleaning, for that matter, since his house had started taking on what he called a "deadline" look. He kept meaning to hire someone to come in once a month at least, but he hadn't gotten around to it. "Devon says nothing's changed. She's looking for a new job—and involved with Ted. Practically married."

"That still gives you some time to woo her."

Oz drew back and shot his friend an amused glance. "Woo? Do you know what that means?"

"Here you go," the bartender said, bringing Michael his drink.

Michael thanked her, and the moment she walked away, he glared at Oz.

"Yeah, I know what it means. Look, you're getting a second chance here."

"She's engaged. She might not have the ring on *at the moment* but she'll wear it once she's back in New York. You know it's true."

"He's the wrong guy. Maybe she thinks nothing's changed, but is that really true? We see the path in front of her even if she's blind to it."

"You're sounding surprisingly philosophical."

"Then be grateful I'm sharing my wisdom with you."

"You're insane."

"Okay, fine. But the ladies at my work are good examples. Most all of them were single up until they approached thirty, and then they started dropping like flies. Dev is thirty-*five*, and you can't tell me she isn't thinking time is running out for her. Maybe that's why she's holding on to this guy so tight, even though he's wrong for her."

"I have no control over her walking down the aisle to another man."

"You have more than you think," Michael countered. "Look, you can't tell me that in all the years of living in that house, Devon didn't hear things. See things. What if, subconsciously anyway, she saw the way Richard treated her mom. What if she thinks that's normal?"

"That's a lot of what-ifs," Oz said, pondering his friend's words. Could it be true? "And I have a book due that I need to work on. I should get home."

He lifted his hand to get the bartender's attention and asked for a box. He might not be hungry now, but come midnight when he took a break, he knew he would be. Writers weren't known for keeping normal hours.

"Oz, come on. Just... play the romantic while she's here. Show her the difference."

"The difference?" Oz asked.

"Between what she has—and what she could have with you. Can't be that hard, right?"

―――――――

THAT SAME EVENING, Devon was in the kitchen making tea when she heard a noise behind her.

"Make one for me, too?" her mother asked.

"Of course. What are you doing up? It's late."

"When you sleep the day away, it means not sleeping at night."

The microwave dinged and Devon removed the mug of water, carrying it to her mother and shoving the tea box across the island toward her. Devon moved to a cabinet and took out another mug, starting the process again.

"Are you all right, dear? You seem— Oh! Aren't you supposed to start your new job tomorrow?"

Devon stared at the numbers on the microwave and used it as an excuse to not have to look at her mother. "It fell through."

"What happened?"

"It doesn't matter, Mama."

"It does matter. Oh, Devon, it fell through because of me, didn't it?" her mother asked, sounding horrified.

"It's fine. It wasn't like I could leave for New York so soon anyway. Especially not with you missing. I'd never be able to forgive myself."

"But I'm home now. And I'm fine."

"Fine?"

Rayna—as her mother said she would now like to be called—stared at Devon with an expression of hurt.

"I'm so sorry I messed things up for you, sweet girl. But, yes, I am fine."

Devon pursed her lips and shook her head in disbelief, her frustration with losing the job, Oz, everything heating up like the water inside the microwave. "So one minute you're running away and endangering your life, but now—everything's just peachy? How is that possible, Mama?"

She felt like a child throwing a tantrum in light of her mother's calm presence, but it was weird, right? The woman had been in a fugue state a little over twenty-four hours ago. And missing!

"It's possible because I've accepted that it's all out of my control. Things happen, Devon, and as hard as they knock us down, we have to get up again and keep living."

"What about Dad?"

"What about him?"

"Are you telling me you've just accepted that he died the way that he did—and you're *okay* with it?"

"Can I do anything to change it?"

"No, but—"

"But nothing. Sweetheart, I lost myself for *days*. Why should I lose more time worrying and complaining about something that will work out one way or the other no matter what I do?"

Okay, so she had a point, but still... "Do you have a plan if the woman's family wins?"

"Not yet, no. But with Connor and Adam's legal help, I'm sure I'll be well represented. The rest is in God's hands."

So calm. How could she be *so* calm? Was her mother in complete denial?

"Devon, I know you don't understand this change in me."

"No, I don't."

"But it's a *good* change. Last night on the water, I finally remembered to be grateful. I'm healthy, I have two beautiful girls, a sister, and friends who love me and mean the world to me— I'm *blessed*, Devon."

"You're okay with losing everything?"

"I'm grateful to have the means to pay the family should I have to."

"Wow."

"I know. It's hard to think in that way, but I have to focus on what I have and not on everything else. I *choose* to focus on the good in my life."

The microwave had beeped a full thirty seconds ago and now reminder beeps had Devon yanking the door open and retrieving her mug.

"How about," her mother said, "we talk about you?"

"I'd rather not."

"Sweetheart, you lost a job because of me. I can tell you're angry."

Devon dunked her tea bag and sighed, shifting her attention back to her mother. "I'm not angry, per se, just... disappointed."

"I don't suppose there's a way you could get it back?"

"No, I don't think so. But even if I could, I don't want to leave you like this. It's too soon, especially with the lawsuit pending."

"Honey, lawsuits take months, sometimes *years* to iron out. Exactly," her mother said when she saw Devon's expression. "Which is why I certainly don't want you to go, but I do understand if you have to. Even though I wish you'd stop running away."

"You're the runaway, Mama, not me."

"Oh, sweetheart, you took off first."

Devon released a huff. "Dara's doing her own thing. Why aren't you saying this to her?"

"Because she didn't have a wedding booked and a dress hanging on her closet door."

Devon cradled her mug to warm her cold fingers. "I knew you and Daddy weren't as okay with me calling it off as you said you were."

"Only because I could see how much you love Oscar."

"Loved," she corrected.

Her mother's silence demanded another glance, and this time Devon shifted uncomfortably at the knowing expression on Rayna's face. "I don't love him," she said, hearing the lie in her tone. "I mean... Mama, Oz is great. He's... wonderful. But he's Saturdays on the beach and picket fences and kids and—"

"And?"

"Living *here*," she said, lifting her hands to indicate the area as a whole.

"You love the beach. And forgive me if I'm wrong, but won't you have to eventually leave the city if you marry Ted?"

She would. Eventually. The governor's mansion was located in Albany, not New York City. And while she could transfer to a network station there, as the governor's wife, would she be able to? Allowed?

And if he wants to run for president?

"Exactly. Which begs the question of why. *Why* are you shortchanging yourself, Devon? You seem so willing to sacrifice your dreams for a man who will never make you a priority."

"Mama, I'd really rather not talk about this right now."

"Because you know I'm right."

"Because you're one to talk about not being a priority," Devon countered, anger getting the best of her.

"I speak from experience. Oh, honey, don't you see? All of this is *why* I don't want you following in my footsteps."

"I'm not."

"You are if you marry someone who will *always* expect you to be the one to sacrifice. You think you won't become me, but stepping into Ted's shadow is doing just that."

Devon didn't speak. Couldn't find the words to counter her mother's argument.

"I've done you and Dara a grave disservice all of these years because I've made you afraid to love."

"I think you're exaggerating, Mama. I love Ted," Devon said, knowing she sounded defensive but unable to help it. Why was everyone so critical of her relationship with him? Why were they trying to ruin things for her?

"Caring for someone and loving them are two entirely different things."

Devon felt flushed from the upset coursing through her, but given all that her mother had been through, she knew she couldn't truly speak her mind.

"For far too many years, I didn't have love, Devon. I have been so lonely, no matter how many things I did to fill the void. Is that the life you want?"

"Isn't that love? Isn't compromise the key to every relationship?"

"Not when one person does all of the compromising. Devon, I loved your father to his dying day, but I should've ended our relationship years ago when he refused counseling, *refused* to give up his lovers."

"Why didn't you?"

"Because I didn't love or believe in myself enough to protect us when I *should* have. Because I thought if I stayed, it would get better, but it didn't. You already know what lies ahead of you. Are you so willing to throw away your dreams?"

In an instant her mind flashed a comparison between Oz and Ted. How, to be a politician's wife, she'd lose that chunk of her identity entirely, whereas Oz—

She gulped the tea, burning her tongue in the process. Her eyes teared as a result. "Oz and Ted aren't interchangeable, Mama."

"No, they're not. But he still loves you and I know you love him, too. Devon, just think about it. Think about what you're giving up in a world where few people get happy endings."

Devon opened her mouth but couldn't come up with another defense. She didn't have one.

Her mother's argument was surprisingly concrete and left Devon struggling.

With Oz... When she was with him, she found herself lowering her guard even as she reeled from fear. Fear that it would become too much. That if she let herself love him again, one day she'd wake up and discover he'd—

Act like her father? Leave her?

And then she really would be her mother. Devastated. Unable to cope. Lost. Because she knew just how devastated she'd been when Oz hadn't followed her to New York. She'd ached for him to come to her. To realize how important it was for her to take the internship.

But he hadn't. And it had taken ten long years

for that ache to lessen to the point of being bearable. To let Ted in.

But was that it?

Was she afraid of giving up control? Afraid of really, truly, loving someone?

Look what happens when you do, she thought, staring at her mother.

Upset settled deep in her stomach. She wasn't the type to back down from a challenge. She wasn't.

But wasn't that what she planned to do? Choose the safer man—just to keep her heart from breaking so badly again?

———

RAYNA DRESSED with care two days later for her first official meeting with Adam Shipley and Connor Sennett.

She was well aware of how she'd appeared to the two men on previous occasions, but she was now ready to show them the new and improved Rayna.

She chose a jean capri pant that hugged her slim body and a beautiful teal top that highlighted her coloring. That done, she added leopard print flats, a necklace, and earrings, and carefully made up her face to disguise the shadows still beneath her eyes.

She wasn't thirty anymore. Or forty. But that didn't mean she couldn't look nice. And after everything Richard had put her through, looking nice boosted her self-esteem and bolstered her confidence even more.

Rayna squirted a hint of perfume and gathered her purse to leave the bedroom. She walked by the double doors to Richard's room without a glance and kept going until she found her girls in the kitchen.

Dara worked on her laptop, no doubt remotely catching up on the work she missed in her office, while Devon waited on toast to pop. "Good morning, girls."

Devon and Dara both turned in her direction, their reactions priceless.

"Wow."

"Mama, you look beautiful."

"Thank you. Every day I feel a little better."

"Scrambled eggs and toast?" Devon asked.

Rayna settled herself at the counter beside Dara and shook her head at the complicated screen in front of her. There were multiple charts, graphs, and a slew of things Rayna couldn't begin to understand. "Big case?"

"Mmm. Yes."

"But you can't talk about it?"

Dara shook her head and closed the laptop. "Nope. Oh, gimme," Dara said, holding out both hands toward Devon, who now held two coffee cups.

Devon passed them off and retreated to get one for herself.

"So, Mama, are you ready for this meeting?" Devon asked.

"As ready as anyone could be. And, girls, I know you're determined to come with me, but if you have other things to do—"

"We don't," they said in unison.

Devon served breakfast next, and then the three of them had a quiet meal, discussing the upcoming weekend activities on the island.

"Let's do the movie by the lake," Dara said. "I loved going to those as a kid."

"I wouldn't mind some time on the beach," Devon added. "We could go to the south end. Maybe it would be a little less crowded."

"I can't wait to do both of those things with you," Rayna said. "But first, Adam and Connor."

"Sounds like a plan. Let's eat up and get over there so we can get started on some fun," Devon said.

Thirty minutes later, the trio walked into Adam and Mary Elizabeth's home. Mary Elizabeth hugged

Rayna tightly before releasing her for Adam to give her a side hug.

"We're so glad you're home safe," the kind man said to her.

She smiled and nodded. "Thank you. All of you. I've become very aware of how blessed I am to have you in my life."

"Even me?" Connor asked, smiling.

Rayna chuckled and felt herself flush a bit, taking a step toward the man to give him a hug as well. "Even you."

If she wasn't mistaken, Connor's gaze lingered a moment longer than it probably should have, and she cleared her throat and stepped back, hoping no one else noticed the heat she felt flooding her face.

"Shall we get started?" Adam asked, stretching out his arm to indicate the living room. "My office would be a little crowded with all of us in it, so I thought we'd meet in here."

Rayna Jo walked into the room beside Dara and noticed Mary Elizabeth's coffee table was covered with papers and files and a laptop. "You've been busy."

"We both have been," Adam said. "Connor has been doing quite a bit of research himself."

She took a seat on the long, tufted couch, her

gaze shifting to Connor once again. "I can't thank you enough."

"My pleasure," Connor said. "I'm not fond of cases that punish a family for an individual's actions."

"So," Adam said, drawing their attention once everyone had seated themselves. "Where would you like to start?"

CHAPTER THIRTEEN

Two days later, Devon stared down at the phone she held in her hand, trying and failing to hide the glee she felt at securing an interview. "I'll be there," she said, noting the time and date. "I look forward to seeing you again."

"If something changes, just give me a call," Stewart Tolliver said. "I hated to hear about you losing the anchor position due to your circumstances, but hopefully we can get you back on the air soon."

"That sounds *wonderful*. Have a good day," she said, returning the man's goodbye before ending the call.

She flopped back in her father's office chair, legs sprawled, arms hanging over the arms and head back as she celebrated the breakthrough.

Finally.

After cold-calling half of New York because she wasn't quite big enough to have an agent, she'd finally secured a face-to-face.

Score one for the small-town girl, she mused.

Her phone began vibrating, and she pressed a finger to answer on speaker. "Devon Teeks."

"Devon, it's been a long time," an oddly familiar voice said.

"I'm sorry, who is this?"

"Georgette Love, from General Broadcasting."

"Georgette! Oh, my goodness, it's so good to hear from you. How are you?" she asked, remembering the woman from ten years ago when she'd worked at the local network.

"I'm doing great. But I'd be doing a lot better if I could lure a certain someone back home."

Devon frowned and sat back in the chair once more. "Pardon?"

"Girl, you know how small our journalistic world is. Word gets around."

She grimaced at the statement. "I suppose it does."

"Well, since you're here and that other job fell through, how about you come work for me?"

Completely flummoxed, Devon didn't know

what to say. "I'm not... I live in New York now, Georgette."

"Come on, a coastal Carolinian in that concrete jungle?"

"It's busy and chaotic," she said, "but I like it."

"I'm offering you your own show. All the bells and whistles. You'd be a big fish in small pond rather than just another in the rat race."

Devon bit her lower lip and stayed quiet, the lure more than she could comprehend.

"Perhaps we could go a *little* higher on pay," Georgette said, her tone coaxing. "Match what you were making in the big city?"

"You don't know what I make."

"I have a good guess. And I'm willing. Are you?"

"I... I don't know what to say."

"Say yes, and it's all yours."

"Georgette, I'm practically engaged to a New Yorker."

"Will you at least think about it?"

Willing to put off the awkward conversation for as long as possible just to get some breathing room, Devon nodded. "I'll think about it, sure. Just don't get your hopes up."

"Already up, my dear. Sky-high and flying. Stop by sometime. Things have changed a lot in ten years, and we have big plans for the right person. If she's willing to take on the challenge, that is. You'll be pleasantly surprised if you give us a chance, Devon. We're a rapidly growing city in need of leveling up."

After chatting a few more minutes, Georgette was called to a meeting and said her goodbyes. Devon thanked her for the offer and ended the call.

"Did I just hear that right?" Dara asked, swinging into the doorway like she'd had her shoulder propped against the frame all this time.

Devon glared at her sister. "Eavesdropping?"

"I didn't want to interrupt."

"It wouldn't have mattered anyway."

Dara glanced behind her into the hallway before walking into the den and closing the door behind her.

"Yeah, right. I know what I heard and you've got to take it."

"I don't have to do any such thing. Why would I?"

"Dev—"

"Dara," she said just as gravely. "I have an interview in New York next week. That'll give me plenty of time to make sure Mama's okay before I head back."

"Obviously she isn't okay," Dara argued. "She

went from totally spacing out to being totally Zen. It's *weird*."

"Then you uproot your work life, quit your current assignment, and come back to stay with her," Devon countered. "See? Problem solved."

"You're seriously turning down your own show?"

She opened her mouth to argue but gave up and switched tactics. "I may be getting *married* or did you forget?"

"I'd certainly like to."

"Dara!"

"He's the wrong guy for you," Dara muttered.

Devon couldn't stop the angry gasp that escaped, and her sister quickly raised her hands as though in surrender.

"Fine. It's none of my business. Even though it is."

"How do you figure that?"

"Am I the only one with the twin thing? I *feel* you, Dev. You're not happy. You haven't been for a long time."

"That's not true."

"Isn't it?" Dara asked with a bold stare.

Devon faltered beneath her twin's perusal, but no matter how much she wanted to argue, she couldn't. "I love New York."

"So visit every now and again. And it's funny, though, how you bring up loving New York instead of your boyfriend. That's telling, don't you think?"

Devon sat back in the leather chair, the scent of her father's cigars wafting to her nose. "You're nitpicking something you know nothing about."

"I know a jerk when I meet one."

"*Dara.*"

"You've been through hell with Mama, and everyone has been here for you—except for him."

"He *was* here."

"For what? An hour? Two? Yet at the first hint of trouble, he bolted for the door."

"He had to get back for a gala I was *supposed* to attend with him. And he had a luncheon the next day."

Dara crossed her arms over her chest and glared, but Devon glared back.

"So you're okay with being Mama in that weird little scenario? Letting Ted *do* whatever he likes while you're left accepting whatever pieces he throws you?"

"Don't you dare stand there and—"

"Fine. I won't," Dara said, yanking open the door. "But years from now, when you're more miserable than ever, remember you have no one to blame but yourself."

DEVON STAYED in the office long after Dara departed because it took that long to regain control of her anger.

Her mind replayed the argument until she wanted to pull her hair out from frustration.

Why did Dara think *she* should be the one to drop everything and move back? Dara had worked remotely the entire last week. She could keep doing that until her assignment was over and she returned to Wilmington.

But, no, Devon was supposed to give up New York and Ted and move back to the island?

Desperate for some comfort, she called Ted and waited for him to answer. "Pick up, come on."

The call went to voicemail, and Dara's statement about accepting whatever time Ted gave her came to the forefront once again as she hung up.

Her phone chimed and she looked at the screen to see Ted's face. He'd called her back. And the fact it meant so much was... kind of sad. "Ted, hi."

"Hi, yourself. Did you get a good response from Stewart?"

Taken aback, she hesitated. "Yes, but... How do you know about that? I just got off the phone with him a little while ago."

"I made some calls," Ted said. "Justin pointed out that it would help to have you back on camera leading up to the vote."

So once again he'd pulled strings, and her call hadn't even been necessary? "I thought Justin didn't like me," she said dryly, "considering my family drama."

"He wants what's best for me, Devon. It's his job. You can't blame him for getting antsy with every-thing happening there."

"Yes, well, it's still going on, so what's changed?"

"You got Connor Sennett involved, that's what. No way would he take the case if he didn't think he could win it. The fact that he's made such a name for himself both in the courtroom and as a writer defi-nitely helps."

"How do you... *How* do you know about Connor? I haven't talked to you since that happened," she said, irritated in the extreme that Ted hadn't called her back despite her voicemails. She'd only received a few texts of *can't talk, going into a meeting, at an event.*

His low chuckle sounded in her ear.

"Don't be upset with me, sweetheart. With everything happening there, Justin thought it would be best to keep someone around."

"What does that mean?" she asked. "Ted, do you have someone *watching* me?"

OZ LIFTED his glass toward the computer screen in front of him, toasting the rough draft of the book finished two full days ahead of his deadline.

With Rayna back home safe, he'd thrown himself into writing, both to meet his goal and to focus on something other than the woman driving him crazy for the second time in his life.

The last half of the draft had rolled from his mind, his fingers flying to keep up the pace. His gut told him he'd produced a solid story, though, and other than a quick read through to find misspellings or dropped words due to the rush of typing, he was good to go.

His gaze shifted from the screen to the window facing the beach and the Atlantic, zeroing in on

Devon as she walked down the boardwalk to the bridge leading over the dunes to the sand.

Her shoulders looked tight, her body language stressed.

He picked up his phone and texted her. *Just finished a rough draft. Come celebrate with me? I'll drive us to the south end for some time on the sand.*

He hit send and then lifted his gaze to watch as she paused and removed her phone from her pocket to check it seconds later.

She stared at the screen a long moment, then lifted her head and looked toward his house as though sensing his gaze from his third-floor office.

Finally he watched as she tapped on her phone and waited for the three dots on the screen to appear in words.

Is that a good idea?

We're friends, Devon. No matter what. Right?

...

The dots appeared and then disappeared, and he glanced up to find her staring at her screen. Debating?

We go as FRIENDS. Fifteen?

He posted a checkmark on her text but couldn't stop his grin as he jumped up from the desk. He'd play the friend card for as long as needed, but they both knew the truth.

It took no time to change into swim trunks and a muscle shirt before he grabbed a towel and then a cooler.

He stared at the contents of his fridge before grabbing a couple of apples, grapes, cheese, then went to the cabinet for wine and crackers.

Finished, he locked up and jogged down the stairs to the open area below, where he loaded a couple of chairs and the cooler in the back of his truck.

He'd just finished when Devon appeared.

"Congratulations on finishing."

"Thanks. Getting to the end always feels good." He took in her tense form and wondered at the cause. Maybe the realization they'd never just be friends? "Is this all you need?"

"Yup," she said, handing over her beach bag and a small cooler.

She was dressed in cutoff shorts he'd guess belonged to Dara and a tank top over her bathing suit.

"I like the hat," he said, eyeing the fifties-style straw fedora.

"Thanks," she said. "I borrowed some things from Dara," she said, confirming his thoughts.

Silence followed and his suspicions rose even more. "What's got you tied up in knots?"

"Nothing."

"There's obviously something. Did Rayna get news about the lawsuit?" he asked.

"No."

"Hey... Dev?" he asked, stretching out a hand to touch her shoulder.

"What, Oz? *What?*"

He held up his hands, palms facing her, and whistled. "Whoa."

She grimaced and turned, and Oz stared at her profile, noting the strong set of her chin, the way her nose arched up a bit at the tip. The rose pink of her lips.

"I'm sorry. Okay? I'm... You're right. I'm in a mood. Sure you want to go anywhere with me?"

"Apology accepted. And, yes, I do. Now what's going on?" he asked, careful to keep his tone neutral.

She turned her head to glance at him but just as quickly turned back to the view.

"I found out today that Ted has someone in town to *keep an eye on me.*"

It took Oz a moment to understand what she

meant. He loaded her gear into the truck, taking a discreet look outside from behind his sunglasses. "Ted has someone spying on you?"

"It appears so, yes."

"Ah. I get it."

"What do you get?"

"Now that you know, you're worried this person saw us kissing that day." He wouldn't mind if they had. In fact—

"No. I mean, it wouldn't be good, but I pushed you away and stopped it and—I think maybe it started after that day," she said. "Ted didn't... He didn't say anything about that. Maybe I should tell him? Be forthright about it?"

"Well, like you said, I kissed you, Devon. I'm the one at fault."

Devon winced and inhaled.

"It's just the thought of someone watching me, you know? It's creepy."

"You do realize that'll be the norm if you marry the guy."

The look of horror on her face told him she hadn't actually thought of the fact politicians living in the spotlight often had security details.

"Did you tell Ted you didn't like it?"

"He said it was for my safety."

A part of Oz could see why the man was concerned about that, but at the same time, he didn't feel that was the actual concern. "Well, unless this person has a four-wheel drive, they won't be following us out onto the sand."

She smiled at that. "They won't, will they? What are we waiting for?"

DEVON LEFT the ocean and made her way across the hot sand to her towel, dropping onto her knees before sliding down on her stomach.

"Feel good to cool off?" Oz asked.

She bit back the moan of relief at getting her body temperature lowered and merely nodded her head. She'd gone with Dara and her mother to the beach a few days ago, but the hour had been spent talking about topics much too serious for relaxation.

But this?

Oz had driven them way out on the south end of the island. With it being a weekday, this part of the beach was mostly deserted, with only a few vehicles in sight.

And those were there when they'd arrived, she

mused, smiling at the fact her spy would be hard-pressed to get pictures now.

Better still, Oz hadn't forced conversation, so she'd been able to lose herself in the sound of the waves crashing against the shore, the heat of the sun on her skin, and call of seagulls overhead. It was the best music and a balm for the soul.

"Hey. You need some sunscreen," Oz said.

She opened one sun-exhausted eye and stared at her skin. With the heat on her back drying the moisture, she didn't want to move. "It's fine."

"It's not fine. You don't want to burn."

"I can't move, though. This is perfect," she said, closing her eyes again.

She didn't hear Oz get up, but something made her aware of his presence beside her. She forced her lashes up once more and watched as he plucked her sunscreen from the top of her bag.

Not a good idea, her mind warned.

Her body didn't care though. She hadn't felt this relaxed and comfortable in... ages. So much so she couldn't actually remember the last time. She'd spent ten years on the go, trying to meet everyone's expectations.

She heard the flip of the bottle cap and braced herself for the squirt of cold lotion. Seconds passed, then Oz's hands settled on her upper back, the lotion warm from his hands as he smoothed it across her shoulders and down her back.

Oz seemed to know just where to press, and she bit her lower lip to keep from moaning when he found tight pressure points and rubbed until her muscles eased. By the time he'd finished applying the sunscreen to her back, neck, and shoulders, she felt like she'd melted into a pile of trembling goo.

And she'd thought she was relaxed before?

"Want me to do your legs?"

Yesss. "N-no. Thank you."

"My pleasure."

The low timbre of Oz's voice revealed more than it disguised, and she realized he still sat beside her on the sand. "Would you... Do you need lotion?"

Maybe she was playing with fire, but seeing as how they were there alone, it was the kind thing to do. Neighborly.

"Yeah. Thanks."

Devon reluctantly pushed herself to her knees and knelt on the towel, grateful her sunglasses and hat hid her face somewhat.

She started on his neck at his hairline and then applied the lotion with efficient motions meant to get the job done quickly. She tried hard not to notice the muscles bulging in his arms and shoulders, the lean ridges of his back.

Unlike his version of lotion spreading, she didn't seek out pressure points or let her hands linger. "There," she said, having to stop and clear her throat when the word emerged silent the first time. Thankfully he didn't see how much touching him... "Done."

She turned and settled herself on the towel once more, applying more lotion to her legs to give herself breathing room and enable her to keep her head down, eyes focused.

"Do you ever think about it?" Oz asked.

"About what?"

"You. Me. If we'd gotten married, we'd have celebrated our tenth anniversary in June."

The waning sunlight still held eighty-five-degree heat with the breeze, and she blamed that on the fire scorching her face as the images of what-if pummeled her. Ten years of marriage. Of birthdays and Christmases—kids? "I... Not really," she said. "Since it didn't happen, I haven't given it much thought."

It was a lie. Whenever she'd thought about kids and settling down, Oz's face often appeared in her mind's eye.

And when she thought of marrying Ted?

She'd wanted nothing more while in New York, but after her time here... the more she thought about it the more her unease grew.

"Have you selected a date for marrying Ted? Are you having kids right away? Getting a house in the suburbs?"

"Can we talk about something else?"

"Most brides-to-be love sharing the details," he said.

"With their ex-fiancés?" she asked. "Seems a little cruel."

"Maybe. But we're friends now, so you can tell me anything."

What was his deal? Why did Oz want her to tell him about her relationship?

Unless... "Maybe we should be getting back."

"Tired of the quiet?"

"I like the quiet," she said, turning to lie on her belly once more. "But I don't like being grilled about Ted."

Oz lay down as well but propped himself on his side, facing her. She could feel his gaze on her. "Stop staring."

"It's hard to look away."

"Oz."

"*Devon*," he said, mimicking her tone with his husky one. "You're beautiful."

She propped her cheek on her folded hands and studied him from behind her sunglasses. "And you're a flirt."

"Only with you."

He propped his head on one arm and lay on his side, looking at her.

"Do you have any idea how badly I want to kiss you again?"

"Oh, Oz. We should leave. I'm—"

"Determined to marry the wrong guy," he quickly interjected. "And I can't stop asking myself why. What are you afraid of? What are you running from?"

"I'm not."

"You are. You did it ten years ago and you're doing it now. I get close and you—"

Devon watched as his expression tightened just a bit, changed, as though he'd stumbled upon the answers to the questions he asked. But if he had, that meant—

"You're afraid to be with me."

"Don't be ridiculous," she said, shoving herself upright and grabbing the T-shirt she'd tossed aside. She yanked it over her head. Where were her shorts?

"You're afraid to love me," he continued. "I threaten you. The question is why?"

"Are all writers as melodramatic as you are right now?" she asked.

Oz reached out and grasped her arm in his hand, tugging just when she was about to shove herself to her feet. It put her off-balance, and she tumbled sideways toward him, landing on his chest. He wrapped his arms around her and rolled so that she was beneath him on her back, legs curled over his side. "O—"

His mouth covered hers, the kiss smothering the sound of his name. She froze hands trapped between their bodies. He softened his hold, tilted his head, and kissed her once more before raising his head and nuzzling his nose against hers.

"Ten years and the ground still shakes when you kiss me."

"Y-you kissed m-me."

Oz's lips curled in a grin that made her body clench.

"Yes, I did. Want me to do it again?"

"I've got an interview in New York in a couple of days," she blurted, desperate to stop the desire she felt for him to kiss her again. "And Ted is waiting for me when I return."

His expression darkened, and Oz drew back, releasing her. He rolled onto his back and stared up at the sky, and even though her statements had gained her her freedom and stopped the kiss exactly as she'd wanted, she felt bereft at the loss.

CHAPTER FOURTEEN

Somehow, someway, Devon managed to extract herself from Oz's embrace without another kiss. Not that she didn't want one.

And the fact she considered herself dating someone else while wanting Oz's kiss left her feeling nauseated. She'd never been that kind of woman. Ever.

Which meant she had to make a decision and fast.

"Can't sleep?" Rayna asked as she left the house and joined Devon outside on the porch. "What's wrong, baby girl?"

Devon glanced at her watch. One thirty-two. "You're up again. Something worrying you, Mama?"

"I asked you first."

Her mother settled in on the porch swing beside Devon and silently accepted half of the throw Devon had brought with her to combat the cooler night breeze.

"Talk to me. You've been very quiet since you got back this afternoon. Did you and Oz argue?"

"How do you know I was with Oz?"

"You are an open book where that man is concerned."

"If that's the case," she murmured, "read me and tell me what I'm doing."

"Okay, I will. You are realizing you still love him," her mother said without pause. "Oh, I don't doubt you have feelings for Ted, too, but Oz has and always will be special to you."

Devon wanted to argue the statement but couldn't. The time on the beach yesterday, his kiss, his touch as he rubbed lotion on her, she'd analyzed every second of it. Overthought every moment. "My life is in New York, Mama."

"Life is where you make it, sweetheart. If you're happy there, fine, but I watched you on *What's Hot* and... maybe I'm just a worrying mother, but you didn't—don't—seem happy."

"There at the end, ratings were down. I was stressed."

"It's more than that, sweetheart. It's Ted—and Oscar?"

Ever since they'd packed the truck up and driven home in complete silence, Devon had struggled. "I have an interview in New York," she said, avoiding the subject. "I'm going to fly out day after tomorrow... Actually, no. I think I'd like some time alone. I'm going to change my ticket and go back early."

Maybe some time in her apartment, surrounded by her things, would help ground her? Allow her to see things more clearly?

"Well, I hate for you to go but I understand."

Devon could hear the disappointment in her mother's voice before Rayna pasted on a smile and patted Devon's hand.

"You'll get the job. I know you will. If that's what you want."

If? *If?* Of course it was what she wanted. Why would she ever want to come back to Carolina Cove? The traffic and tourists during the season were nearly as bad as New York City!

"I had a visitor today," Rayna said.

"One of the Babes?" Devon asked.

"No. It was Connor."

Was her mother blushing?

"He stopped by to check on me and give me an update on the lawsuit."

"Adam Shipley could've done that," Devon said, studying her mother's changing expressions.

"Yes, well, Connor just wanted to make sure everything had sorted itself out with the kayak, too."

"I see." Devon stared up at the moon, wondering when it had become normal for her mother to talk about a man other than her father. But it had. And it was good. "Mama? Did Logan and Zoey get you into therapy? I'm just asking because of everything going on, maybe it's not the best time to have a crush on one of your attorneys?"

"Oh, Devon, I have no such thing. Connor is a friend. Just like Oz is your friend."

Devon thought of the kiss on the beach. How she'd wanted nothing more than for it to continue even though...

"Mama, can I ask your advice?"

"Of course."

"Oz... kissed me. Yesterday."

"I wondered if it was something like that."

"It was just a kiss but... should I tell Ted? I mean, he's my boyfriend and he wants to marry me when things settle and—"

"This happened on the beach?"

"Yes—and... the other day. At the pier. *Oz* kissed *me* both times but—"

"Did you want him to kiss you?"

Oh, now, that was the question, wasn't it?

"Never mind," Rayna said. "I know the answer to that. Oh, Devon, I hate the turmoil I've caused you."

"To be fair, Dad technically started it," Devon muttered.

"Yes, well, you're still here because of me and my memory loss and behavior. I know I'm at least partially to blame for the fact you're so... torn."

"No, Mama, you aren't to blame. I'm just confused. Being here, seeing Oz. It's very strange. It makes it hard to sort out my feelings. To know what's a part of the past a-and what I feel now."

"And Ted?"

Ted. "I'm upset with Ted, which isn't helping."

"I see. Is that why you allowed Oscar to kiss you?"

Was it? "No. Oz surprised me. Both times."

"That boy loves you. Always has. He just can't help himself. Did you punch him?" Her mother laughed softly. "Don't give me that look. I remember when that old college buddy of Logan's tried to kiss you when you and Oscar were engaged. You walloped that boy good."

She had totally forgotten that. And he'd felt her right hook, hadn't he? Sported a black eye for a week, too.

"So?" Rayna asked. "Why did Oscar not get the same treatment?"

Why not, indeed?

"Oh, sweetheart. Can I offer some advice?" her mother asked.

"I wish you would," Devon said, bracing herself just in case.

"Go to New York."

"What?" Of all the things her mother could've said, that wasn't what she'd expected.

"Go to New York," Rayna said again. "To the interview. To your apartment. Go out with Ted and let him kiss you."

"O-kay. Why?"

"Well, the first time you left, you ran away. Now, let me finish," Rayna said when Devon opened her mouth to argue. "You ran away because you had a dream, and you just weren't ready to settle down. But this time you're running back to what you want. To the home you've made for yourself. I think once you're there, one way or another, that will tell you everything you need to know."

She wasn't so sure. What if she got there and she was just as torn and mixed up as she felt here?

OZ PACED his kitchen floor until the timer he'd set dinged, alerting him to the fact it was a decent hour go to calling at someone's door.

He left the house in a rush, his long strides eating up the distance between his house and Rayna Teeks's.

Ever since his time on the beach with Devon, he'd struggled with wanting go caveman, throw her over his shoulder, and keep her locked up somewhere until she came to her senses and realized she belonged there, with him and her family.

But since he couldn't do that—*legally*—he had to settle for appearing on her doorstep like the lovesick puppy he was and hope he could get her to actually listen to him.

Somehow, someway, he'd make it work. Compromise. As a full-time writer, he could work anywhere now. All he needed was a laptop and an unlimited supply of coffee.

New York was a creative city, and while he certainly did not want to live there permanently, he'd be willing to compromise and spend part of the time there. He'd do whatever she wanted, needed, to make it work.

She just had to get rid of Ted and—

"Oscar," Rayna said, opening the door before he could knock. "Good morning. I saw you coming up the steps. Is everything all right? It's so early."

The woman wore her bathrobe, and Oz grimaced at his bad manners. "I know. I'm sorry about that but I need to talk to Devon. Face-to-face."

"Oh," Rayna said. "I'm afraid that's impossible. She's gone. She changed her flight and returned early to have some time before her interview."

Changed her flight? Had their kiss scared her that much? "Is she coming back?"

Rayna gave him a sad look.

"I guess that depends on if she gets the job. Would you like to come in? Have some coffee?"

He didn't respond but he didn't have to. Rayna stretched out a hand to grasp his and pulled him inside, leading the way to the kitchen, where she scooted out a seat at the island.

"Sit, sit. I'll get us fixed right up."

He watched as she quickly found mugs and went to the pot already in the process of filling.

A knock sounded and he turned to see Logan outside the kitchen door. "I'll let him in."

"Thank you, dear."

Logan raised his eyebrows high when Oz unlocked and swung the door wide.

"Hey. What are you doing here?" Logan asked, lowering his voice. "Something wrong with Rayna?"

"No. I, uh, came over to talk to Devon but she's left for New York."

Logan drew back, his expression a combination of sadness and pity.

"Sorry, man."

"Logan, what are you doing here?" Rayna asked her nephew. "Checking up on me again?"

"Just coming to see my favorite aunt," Logan said. "And hoping there might be some breakfast involved."

Logan clapped a hand on Oz's shoulder before he crossed to Rayna and bent to kiss her cheek.

"Scrambled or over easy?" Rayna asked.

"Scrambled."

"Oscar? Would you like some eggs?" Rayna waved her hand and shook her head. "I'm making you some eggs," she said.

Oz smiled wryly at the statement and found his seat at the island, remembering the days when he, Michael, and Logan were all three lined up waiting for their plates to be filled at one house or another before a day at the beach with all of the pseudo cousins.

"So, she left again huh?" Logan asked softly.

"She has an interview," Oz said. "The past is repeating itself all over again."

"Maybe she won't get it," Logan said.

"Even if she doesn't, she's still with him." *Ted.* He'd have to write a character named Ted in one of his books. Make him a murder victim, Oz mused darkly.

"Oscar," Rayna said, "may I offer some advice?"

He forced himself to meet the woman's knowing gaze and nodded. "I'd appreciate that."

Rayna paused in her breakfast prep to stand opposite them at the island.

"How willing are you to fight for my daughter?"

"I'm willing to compromise on New York this time if that's what you're asking."

"Seriously?" Logan asked, expression one of surprise. "I thought you hated it there."

"I wouldn't want to live there year-round but... if

it's that important to Devon, maybe we could split our time between there and here."

"That is a very good start," Rayna said, nodding. "Have you told her this?"

"No. I was going to this morning but—"

"But she's already gone. Well, perhaps a phone call? Or one of those video chats since you wanted to speak to her in person?"

Not exactly the way he wanted things to go, but under the circumstances, it might be his only chance. "Maybe."

A knock sounded on the door, and he turned to find the rest of the Boardwalk Babes waving at them through the windows.

"You having a party, Rayna?" Logan asked.

The woman released an engaging laugh and hurried to the door. "I am now! Girls! Come see my handsome breakfast companions. Would you like some scrambled eggs?"

"We brought breakfast with us," Tessa said.

Oz watched as the Babes entered, carrying towel-draped dishes. In typical motherly fashion, the Babes grabbed plates and utensils and served Oz and Logan heaping spoonfuls of eggs, waffles, bacon, a scone, and fresh fruit.

"You guys covered all the bases," Logan said to them. "Why am I not surprised?"

Adaline kissed and hugged Logan.

"Because you know we love our food while we chat. Oz? Are you okay?" Adaline asked, bringing everyone's attention to him.

Oz felt his face heat at the multitude of stares, and he nodded. "Fine. Hungry. This is delicious."

"Devon left this morning for New York," Rayna said, spoiling his excuse.

Within seconds, Oz found himself surrounded by the women in one big group hug that left Logan failing to disguise a chuckle. "I'll be fine," Oz said to them.

"Of course you will," Adaline said.

"And if she doesn't come back, it's her loss," Tessa said, earning a frowning look from Rayna. "Well, it's true. Oz is wonderful."

Rayna squeezed his arm and nodded. "I whole-heartedly agree. You're one of us, no matter what."

One of them... just not the way he wanted to be.

DEVON TOOK a taxi from the airport to her apartment and smiled tiredly at the security officer sitting behind his desk on her walk to the elevator.

She hoped to sneak in a nap before going to see Ted, especially since she'd slept so little the night before.

The elevator ride to her floor seemed to take forever, but finally she arrived. Devon stepped off and turned to pull her suitcase over the break from the elevator to the floor when movement caught her eye. She lifted her head, noting Mrs. Luiz... leaving *her* apartment?

Devon ducked out of sight and discreetly watched the woman hurry down the hall and silently enter her own apartment. The door shut without a sound other than a soft *snick* of the lock.

Stomach in knots, Devon hefted her suitcase so it couldn't be heard rolling down the hallway and quietly made her way to her apartment door. Her heart pounded in her chest and her palms felt sweaty with unease. Why was Mrs. Luiz in her apartment?

The apartment door was unlocked, and Devon left her suitcase outside and quietly twisted the knob to let herself in, holding her breath as though that would combat any noise she might make.

Rose petals coated the floor of her entry and led

to her living area. Two champagne glasses sat on her coffee table beside the unopened and chilled bottle. And that sat beside a bouquet of at least three dozen blood red roses.

Tiptoeing through the living room, she stood frozen and took it all in. There were flowers on every surface, on her kitchen countertop. More on her dining table. Candles were lit and gently flickering as the wicks burned. It was beautiful. Romantic. Very much something her event planner neighbor could have pulled off with a few hours' notice and Ted's credit card.

Her inhalation was audible, and she clamped a hand over her mouth to squelch it and forced herself to keep going, knowing that with each step she took she tread closer to a decision she'd pondered during her flights to New York. The decision she so desperately needed to make and yet—couldn't.

"Ah, sweetheart, I missed your entrance," Ted said as he emerged from the bedroom.

He carried a lighter in his hand and wore a grin that melted her heart.

"I wanted to surprise you and show you how much I've missed you."

"It's...beautiful. I can't believe you did this."

"Well, you mentioned your friend could probably use the business and I wanted to do something special to mark your return to civilization so... What do you think? You like?"

"It's amazing." Over the top. Only Ted would go to such lengths.

"Good. Oh, but there's something missing."

Food? Her stomach rumbled and of all the things that came to mind, that was it. Though probably not what he—

"This."

Ted pulled a familiar blue box from his inner jacket pocket and closed the distance between them. She couldn't hold his gaze and glanced away, panic rolling over her, and as she took in the flowers and candles with a sweep of her gaze she realized it meant—nothing. She could appreciate the sight of it. The beauty and effort. But instead of feeling joy or elation or *passion*—she only felt unease. Dread. And didn't that tell her everything she needed to know?

The knot in her stomach grew bigger than ever and her mother's words came to mind and she knew —*knew*—this was what she'd meant. This was why her mama had urged her to come back to New York. So that when she saw Ted and didn't feel like a girl-friend should... didn't feel the excitement knowing he was about to propose again...how could she ever marry him?

"Goes right—"

"No." She snatched her hand away before he could take hold of it and slide the ring on her finger. Heat suffused her cheeks and tears filled her eyes but she couldn't let him finish. Couldn't go back to that night weeks ago when he'd proposed and she'd said yes and meant it. She had meant it then. But now? "I can't. Ted, I'm sorry. I'm so sorry, but...I can't."

Ted stiffened and straightened to his full height, nostrils flaring as he inhaled and stared at her hard.

"I see. Does this have anything to do with Oscar Roman?"

"Because it wouldn't be right," she insisted. "Ted, the time away made me realize a lot of things about myself. Good and bad. Most importantly, it made me realize I can't be the woman you want."

"You don't know what you're talking about."

"I do. You like who I am now for the advantages I bring to the table, but what about later?"

"What about it?"

"Ted, I don't want to give up my life and career to be a politician's wife. I haven't worked as hard as I have to just—stop. I love what I do. Who I am.

And...*she* isn't someone I can compromise. Not after the battle I've had to get here."

Ted swallowed hard, his Adam's apple moving up and down in a visible gulp.

"Devon, we can work through this. Is this because I didn't make it to the funeral?"

"No. I mean, you not being there factors in, but it's more that it drew attention to the fact that down the line, if we were to marry, you wouldn't be there for me then either."

"You're saying I'm selfish."

"I'm saying your career will take priority over everything else. And for some women, that's okay and more power to them. But it's not for me and I don't think I realized it until now." The silence following her words told her everything about his thoughts.

It amazed her. It took time to build a relationship —texts and phone calls, dates and weekends. But it only required seconds to end one. Maybe that was yet another indication of the lack of depth their relationship held?

Ted tucked the ring back into his pocket and moved toward the door without another word. He paused and she braced herself for whatever he was about to say.

He opened his mouth but then closed it, giving his head a tight shake as he pulled his hand from his pants pocket and held up the key she'd given him several months ago. He tossed it into the bowl by the door and walked out.

Devon crossed the rose-petaled floor and softly shut the door behind him. She lowered her head on the wood with a slight bang and closed her eyes to stop the burning.

She'd told Ted the truth about keeping her identity. Wanting more than to disappear into the shadows behind him as the smiling, political wife. But now?

What now?

CHAPTER FIFTEEN

R ayna lifted the lightweight carrier and moved it a few steps farther down the back porch, the weeds inside bouncing when she set it down again.

"You're looking productive today," a voice said from behind her.

She turned and found Connor regarding her with a friendly grin. "Oh, hi. What are you doing here?" she asked as she pulled off her gardening gloves and wished she wasn't covered in a layer of sand and dirt and sweat.

Normally she would've hired a company to weed, but given her uncertain financial future, she tried to cut back wherever she could. Plus, she'd always loved gardening. Richard hadn't considered it appropriate for his wife to be seen in the dirt like a laborer, but she'd always found tending her flowers relaxing.

"I had a meeting with Adam and thought I'd drop by. I have good news for you, and seeing as how Adam had another meeting, I get to be the lucky man who gets to tell you."

"Good news? Really?" She was afraid to get her hopes up too much but... maybe an affordable settlement?

"The family agreed to our offer."

"I made an offer?"

"You entrusted us to work on your behalf, so yes."

"How much?" she asked, barely daring to breathe.

Connor grinned. "For what the insurance companies will pay out. It's a nice sum, and the girls' parents were surprisingly reasonable when it came to not fighting for more from you since you were a victim in this."

Her knees felt weak, and she reached behind her, trying to find the edge of the short stone wall so she could sit before she collapsed from relief.

Connor rushed to her side and helped guide her down, and she wrapped her hands around his forearms, squeezing them. "It's real? It's over already?"

"It's over," he said. "They weren't greedy as much as desperate. Their daughter left behind a young child—not Richard's," he added, "and burial expenses. I think they just needed help to stay afloat."

"Oh, Connor." She leaned forward and slid her arms around him, hugging him tight. "Thank you. Thank you, *thank you*. You have no idea what this means to me."

Connor held her for a moment before pulling back, his gaze tender as he stared at her.

"I have an idea. And now that you're not technically a client, would you do me the honor of going out with me?"

Rayna gasped. "Going... A date?" He asked her out when she had to look like a grimy street urchin?

"Yes, a date—my first since my wife passed."

What would people think? Richard had only just passed but... "Yes," she said without giving herself time to form excuses. She and Richard hadn't had a real marriage in years. If people wanted to gossip, let them.

"Yes?"

"Yes," she said firmly, nodding. Smiling. "I don't

care if people talk," she said. "I've never met a man as kind and caring as you."

Connor lifted his hand and lightly ran his knuckles down her cheek.

"I feel the same way about you," he told her. "I'd really like to kiss you, Rayna."

"What's stopping you?"

"We haven't even gone on a date yet," he said, pretending to be shocked.

Rayna laughed, feeling as light and carefree as a schoolgirl with no worries. "Maybe not, but you *have* fixed me breakfast. Surely that counts for something?"

"Well now, I think you're right," he said, moving toward her, his gaze lowering to her lips. "I believe it does."

"SO? WHAT DO YOU THINK?"

Devon blinked to awareness and realized she'd totally zoned out at the end of her interview. Not exactly a good way to make an impression. "It sounds... great."

"So is that a yes?"

She opened her mouth to confirm, but the word

just wouldn't come. So she tried again. And the same thing happened.

"Devon? Is something wrong?"

She inhaled and raked her fingers through her hair, glanced out the windows of his beautiful office facing Rockefeller Center. "I-I know what a wonderful opportunity this is but... can I have a few days to think about it?"

Stewart's shock was evident, as was his displeasure that she didn't immediately agree to his job proposal.

"I suppose we could give you twenty-four hours. If you pass, we'll move on to other candidates who were recommended. I have to ask though. Why the need to think it over?"

Devon inhaled and stood, pacing over to the window to look down at the activity below. A typical day in New York. Busy, bustling. So why didn't it appeal as much now? Just because of what had happened with Ted? "There have been quite a few changes in my life in the last several weeks. I'd just like some time so that I don't feel like I'm making a rushed decision, that's all."

Stewart joined her at the windows, leaning a shoulder against the vertical metal beam lining the glass.

"Devon, it's none of my business, but are you all right? You seem... distracted. Definitely not your usual focused self."

A laugh rumbled out of her chest, and she crossed her arms over her front. "I am distracted," she admitted. "I apologize that it's so obvious."

"Anything I can do to help sort things out?"

Stewart was a handsome man, with dark navy eyes and silvery blond hair. She imagined he got his way quite often with a smile and pretty words. "No. Thank you though."

"Well, if that changes, let me know."

She nodded and turned to hold out her hand, shaking his before following him back to his desk to retrieve her purse.

Devon ignored the receptionist since she was busy on a call anyway and moved across the lounge. A familiar voice drew her attention, and she paused to stare in shock at her former assistant, Tia, onscreen? How did that happen?

"Isn't it great?" the receptionist said as she set the phone on the base. "She's one of my roommates," the girl continued. "I can't believe she scored such a big break. Right place, right time," the young woman said.

Devon agreed with a silent nod and left the

office, and once she was in the lobby of the building, she made her way to the ladies' room. She put her hands under the faucet and let cold water run over them.

Had she really walked out of the meeting without taking the job offer? Wasn't Tia's big move in front of the camera proof that Devon had no time to waste *thinking?*

A woman emerged from a stall and moved to wash her hands.

"Nice tan. You must've been somewhere fun. Oh, hey, aren't you Devon from *What's Hot?*"

Devon pasted her camera-ready smile on her face and nodded. "I am."

"Oh. Wow. I am so sorry about everything. Your dad and your show... But, hey, you've got to go with the flow, right?"

"Right," she repeated, having to bite out the word.

The woman washed her hands and left, and Devon stood there, facing the mirror.

She had to go with the flow.

Like sand with the tide?

BACK AT HER apartment Devon set about cleaning to make use of the surge of energy zipping through her. The rose petals on the floor were the worst to clean up, but she hadn't had the presence of mind or the will to to do the chore yesterday after Ted's departure.

Once those were taken care of, Devon grabbed her cell phone and carried it with her to the window. She opened it and climbed out on the fire escape to sit.

The alley was fairly quiet, but when she looked around, she hated that all she could see were buildings.

The sun was going down, but other than the waning light, she saw nothing of the color. No, the alley was already getting dark, and she heard sirens and truck brakes, car horns and loud bangs. The smell of the dumpster down below her...

Devon glanced at her phone and noted the texts she'd received during her interview. Her mom and Dara, Logan and Zoey—

Oz.

She clicked on them one by one, reading complaints that she'd left without saying goodbye followed by well wishes for her interview. For her happiness. All of the texts ended with love and she felt that love through the digital device.

She'd also missed a call and a video call from Oz, and when she checked her voicemail, she found a message from him as well.

Hey, Devon, I stopped by the house yesterday morning because I wanted to tell you... I wanted to tell you that I'm here for you. Always. Good luck with the interview and with Ted, with everything. I, uh, wish you all the best. Knock 'em dead."

The messaged ended with a click, and Devon lowered the phone and stared out toward the street once again.

When she thought of friends she could contact in New York right now, no one came to mind. Most were acquaintances at best. Not people she could share her problems with and ask for advice. More than anything, they'd probably tell her to work while she could and then stick around for the ride as Ted rose among the political set. That was more important to people who planned their divorce before planning their wedding.

And the interview today? It had gone well. It was a good position in the network, one that could lead to more in time.

So why hadn't she accepted it immediately?

She picked up her phone and hit Dara's number. Her sister picked up on the second ring.

"Hey, how'd it go?"

Devon pressed her fingers to her forehead and rubbed, unable to stop the migraine forming. Her father, her mother, Oz, Ted—

"Dev? You okay?"

She inhaled and shook her head. "No," she said softly, voice thick.

"Oh, no. You didn't get the job?"

"I did."

"O-kay," Dara said, drawing out the word, "so what's up? What's wrong?"

"I think... I think it's just all hitting me."

"Well, that's understandable. We haven't had much time to process things with everything going on with Mama. It's okay. It's understandable."

"Then why aren't you...?"

"Maybe because in the business I'm in, not a lot surprises me anymore."

"You sound jaded."

"I suppose I am. But, hey, it's a good living, I like what I do—I just don't necessarily like the people I'm asked to investigate, you know?"

"Have you investigated... Dad?" Silence followed the question, and Devon stared out at the rapidly darkening alley. "I knew there was a reason you distanced yourself. Why didn't you tell me?"

"Dev—"

"How bad was it?"

"I'm not going to bash the dead. It won't do any good. Oh, hey, I've got good news, too," Dara said before she went on to explain about the settlement with the lawsuit.

"That's great."

"I know, right? I think Mama's about float away she's so happy. You should see her."

"I wish I could."

"You can, you know."

Devon closed her eyes and squeezed them tight. "Ted asked me to marry him again."

"And?"

"I said no."

"Whoa, really?"

"It was everything a girl could want. He surprised me with flowers and rose petals but—I couldn't do it. I couldn't say yes."

"Because?"

"I told Ted it was because of his career and how mine would have to take a backseat eventually."

"I can see that. But why do I get the feeling there's more?" Dara asked.

"Because there is," she whispered. "I just keep thinking about everything and I don't ever want to be in a relationship like that. Like... Mama and Daddy's. I mean, I was about to accept breadcrumbs when..."

"You want the whole dang loaf," Dara said with a soft laugh.

Devon smiled and nodded. "Yeah, I guess I just believe I'm loaf worthy."

"That's because you are," Dara said. "I hated the though of you giving up everything to be a pretty face but I knew it had to be your decision."

"So tell me something—and be honest. What would you do? About the jobs?

Dara's inhalation filled the phone. "Look, Dev, we are very, very different people."

"I know but—I need help here."

"Do you? Because I think you already know the answer."

Devon leaned her head back against the metal rail behind her and stared up at the night sky.

"Look, I support you whatever you decide, okay? I just want you to be happy, Dev. Wherever—with whomever—that means. But you're the only one who can decide *how* this plays out for you."

Devon didn't speak for a long moment, her thoughts racing between possibilities and facts. "The city feels...different now. Not because of Ted but just —different."

"And when you were here? How did it feel?"

She closed her eyes again. "It felt like home."

"But?"

"I don't know. This is home, too? And after leaving the way that I did, moving back to Carolina Cove just seems like... failure," she said.

"Are you kidding me? You were offered your own television show. If you took it, you'd be returning in triumph having made your mark in New York."

She supposed that was one way to look at it. "You think so?" she asked, glaring at the interior of her darkened apartment.

"I know so," Dara said. "Now... what are you going to do?"

ONE MONTH after Devon's departure for New York, Oz walked along the beach, trying and failing to clear his mind for the plotting session he had planned for the day.

It was early, the sun barely making an appearance on the horizon. The beach was nearly deserted with only a few early risers walking the surf, looking for shells, or holding phones ready to capture the sunrise.

He hadn't heard from Devon since she'd left. Not a text, not a phone call. Nothing.

And even though they'd made it through the past breakup, and he'd remained friends with her family, Michael and Logan were now acting weird as well.

Breakups caused tension, but considering he and Devon hadn't actually been together, he was confused by the awkwardness. Maybe it was that she'd turned him down yet again?

Head down, he made his way to the bridge over the dunes. A bit of red caught his eye, and he frowned at the sand. Bending, he picked up the piece of sea glass and got a punch to the gut when he realized it was shaped like a heart.

He ran his thumb over the surface, feeling the smooth edges. A few steps later, he stopped again, spotting another piece of red glass.

Oz lifted his head, gaze moving from one red bit to the next, scattered across the sand leading to the bridge.

Heart pulsing, Oz quickly gathered them up, including the two on the steps, five across the bridge, and more down the steps and boardwalk toward his house?

Could it be?

He was afraid to hope and fought the urge to rush. Instead he forced himself to pick up every piece he saw, shoving them into his pockets.

Pulse pounding, when he crossed the road onto his property, the heart-shaped glass increased in quantity and his hands started to shake. "Devon?" he called, not seeing her.

He left the glass for now and rushed up the steps, only then noticing the open front door.

Devon stood in his living room, beautiful in a long, strapless red sundress that bared her shoulders.

He stopped dead in his tracks, unable to take another step. His mind snapped a mental photo of her so that he'd never forget this moment.

"Hi," she said simply.

"Hi."

"I hope you don't mind. I remembered where the spare key was kept."

He swallowed the fist choking him and forced himself to get to the point. "What's going on?"

Oz watched as she pursed her lips and inhaled.

"I went back to New York."

"I'm aware."

"But nothing was the same. Ted and I... It's over."

"Good."

"Don't hold back."

"You deserve better."

"I think I do," she whispered. "But I'm not sure I'm worthy of the guy I-I like."

He narrowed his gaze, hands fisted to keep himself in check. "He's probably a jerk, too."

"I don't think so."

"Yeah, well, you didn't think Ted was a jerk, either."

A wry laugh emerged from her, and he liked that he was able to draw the sound from her. "What about that job you interviewed for?"

"I got it."

He shoved his hands into his pockets and grabbed hold of the glass, trying to remind himself there was a reason she was here again. "Congratulations."

"Thanks. I didn't take it."

He didn't move, couldn't even take a breath. "No?"

She shook her head, the long braid hanging over her left shoulder moving with the act, drawing his attention to her beautiful skin and the freckles on her shoulders.

"No."

"What's going on, Devon?"

"Oz, I hurt you and I'm sorry. I know it's no excuse, but I had to find my own way a-and figure things out."

"I know."

"No, you don't," she said, taking a step toward him before she stopped. "I thought I had everything I could ever want in New York, but after being here and going back there, I realized how empty it all was. But Ted aside, I knew if I moved back here, it had to be right."

"I see. Maybe you should know I've been doing some thinking myself."

"You have?"

He nodded. "I wasn't willing to compromise ten years ago. I didn't feel like I could leave my dad or my job. This place. But now that Dad's doing better and I'm writing full-time... I can write anywhere. Including New York."

"You'd do that?"

"If it means being able to spend time together, yes. Summers in New York, winters here. We'll make it wor— Wait, did you say *move* back?"

She smiled the most beautiful smile and closed the distance between them. "Hold out your hand."

He did as ordered, more than a little charmed by the effort she was putting into her apology.

He opened his hand, and she took it in one of hers, the other lifting to place a small bag of sand in his palm. Inside was a red heart-shaped piece of glass larger than the others he'd found.

Devon curled his fingers around the bag, his hands wrapped in hers.

"Mama had a point that day," she whispered. "You've always loved me, and I was selfish and took that for granted. I'm sorry."

"What does this mean, Devon?"

Another small smile drew his gaze to her lips.

"The tide has finally shifted. I'm home. And I'd like us to... well, I'd like us to start over, but I understand if you—"

Without warning, he drew her close and lowered his head for a kiss.

"Wait!"

"I don't want to," he grumbled, earning a sweet laugh.

"No, after everything I've put you through, I want to do this right."

"Then hurry up, because I want to kiss you," he

grumbled. "And not have you running away afterwards."

"Oscar Roman," she said in a serious voice that belied the amusement and love he saw in her eyes, "would you do me the honor of dating me again?"

"Yes," he said against her lips. "Now shut up and kiss me."

EPILOGUE

Two weeks later

"Today has been great but that's all for our very first show," Devon said to the camera. "Tune in tomorrow for a fabulous interview with *New York Times* Best-selling Author, Oscar Roman, who'll discuss his latest thriller release and give us a sneak peek into what's coming next. And Julie Ani, the winner of the Food Fantastic competition, will show us basic tricks to ramping up our beach get-togethers to make them not only memorable but delicious, too. Until then, have a great day and enjoy that sunshine."

Devon held her smile until given the all clear and turned to face the group waiting for her backstage. "Well?"

Oz grinned with pride, as did her mother, and Devon hurried across the set toward them.

Oz drew her to him for a quick kiss and then released her for her mother to hug.

"You were wonderful, sweetheart. Just wonderful!" Rayna said, releasing her.

"I agree," Connor added. "Congratulations, young lady. I see a success in the making."

"I couldn't agree more," Georgette said, also giving Devon a quick hug. "You're a natural talk show host."

"Thank you. I'm so glad you kept after me to come back home."

"Well," Connor said. "Shall we go celebrate?"

Her mother smiled up at Connor, and Devon loved the fact her mother looked so happy. Not only looked it but anyone could see she'd fallen madly in love with Connor, and the man with her. Devon wouldn't be surprised if there were wedding bells in their future.

The five of them made their way out of the building. It was a short drive to the elegant oceanfront restaurant, and Devon, Oz, her mother, and Connor chatted the entire way about the plans for her show and future guests.

Once at the restaurant, the group was greeted

warmly by the hostess, and Oz urged Devon to take the lead.

Devon focused on the gorgeous view and not running into chairs along the way, which was why she didn't see the group gathered.

"Congratulations!"

The Babes, their husbands and children, and even a few of the grandchildren lined the table and applauded.

Devon smiled, trying and failing to hide the color surging to her cheeks as the rest of the large restaurant looked on with curiosity. "Thank you. I can't believe you're all here! I'm so glad we can celebrate together."

Her mother and Connor took seats, but when Devon started to pull out a chair, Oz took her hand and stopped her.

She looked up at him in surprise.

"Marry me," he said softly.

Devon gasped. "What?"

Oz narrowed his gaze on her at the response and she hurried to correct it. "You're sure?"

"What are you two whispering about over there?" Michael asked.

"I've never been more sure of anything in my life," Oz said. "Will you marry me?"

Those closest to them heard the question, and a low murmur went through the group. Devon placed her hands on his chest and rose onto her tiptoes, pressing her lips to his. "Yes. Yes, absolutely, yes."

The group let out whoops and applause while Oz wrapped his arms around her and lifted her up against him, kissing her. "I love you," she murmured against his lips. "And this time I promise—I'll race you to the altar."

I hope you enjoyed reading Sea Glass and Second Chances. Up next is Logan and Zoey's story so be sure to preorder SEA BLUE AND LOVING YOU!

SEA BLUE *AND LOVING YOU blurb:*

She's off-limits. That's the first thing Dr. Logan Davenport thinks every morning before going to work at the same hospital as counselor Zoey Barnes. Officially friend-zoned because he can't stand the thought of losing her lifelong friendship, his secret crush can never be revealed. But when Zoey is injured by a patient and Logan realizes how close to the breaking point Zoey actually is, the doctor in him—and the man who loves her more than he should—can't ignore it.

Zoey Barnes is all too aware of the attention her childhood friend receives from others in the hospital. Logan's good looks and bedside manner leave many fawning over him. But when he "kidnaps" her after she's injured and takes her to his mountain retreat to heal, she's the one drawn by his bedside attentions. Still, she's seen what love does to perfectly sane people, and since she's spent her career helping people recover from the pain inflicted by the ones they love, she knows not to let him get too close. Logan calls her forced vacation a sabbatical. She calls it torture. Nature? Resting? Seeing Logan in his swim trunks beneath a waterfall?

After too many days together and far too many salacious thoughts, reality returns with a punch. They finally go home to Carolina Cove but Zoey can't forget exchanging one forbidden what-if kiss. When her patients need her and crashing and burning is one of the many possible outcomes with Logan, can she risk falling in love?

SEA BLUE AND LOVING YOU

BOOKS ALSO SET IN CAROLINA
COVE

CAROLINA COVE SERIES:

- SEASCAPES AND VEGAS MISTAKES
- SEASHELLS AND WEDDING BELLS
- SEA GLASS AND SECOND CHANCES
- SEA BLUE AND LOVING YOU

MAKE ME A MATCH SERIES:

- ROMANCE RESET

- RULES OF ENGAGEMENT
- THE MATCHMAKER'S SECRET
- PERFECTLY MISMATCHED
- BY THE BOOK

THE SEASIDE SISTERS SERIES:

- THE LAST GOODBYE
- LATTES AND LULLABYES
- MAP OF DREAMS
- WORTH THE RISK
- LOST LOVE FOUND

COMING SOON: (LINKS WILL BE UPDATED ASAP)

THE BLACKWELL BROTHERS SERIES:

- BABY BE MINE
- SECOND CHANCE WEDDING
- THE GETAWAY GUY
- OFF-LIMITS LOVE
- FLIRTING WITH FOREVER

Want to read other books set in my fictional coastal town of Carolina Cove? Check out the excerpt of THE LAST GOODBYE:

Dominic Dunn hit his turn signal and waited for a family of five to cross the sidewalk before he turned into the Carolina Cove Inn lot and parked, dread filling his stomach. Just the sight of the happy families and tourists wandering the sidewalks, lounging on restaurant patios, and enjoying the lively Saturday night left him angry. He should've ignored the letter. Ignored his next-door neighbor and best friend, ignored his boss and coworkers who said he had to honor Lisa's last request and come here.

"Mister? You gonna get out?"

The boy's voice startled Dominic and he turned to see a kid around eight years old watching him. The salt-air breeze blowing through the open windows of his car brought with it the smell of fried foods from the restaurants nearby, and seagulls squawked as they flew overhead.

"Mister?"

"Yeah," Dominic said, only then realizing he'd pulled into a parking place and was literally sitting there with his foot on the brake as he debated his choices of whether to throw the new car in reverse and floor it to get out of Carolina Cove as quickly as possible... or stay the prepaid two weeks Lisa had booked for him before her death.

"Doesn't look like it. Are you drunk?"

A rough-sounding chuckle left his chest. "Do you get a lot of drunk people here?"

"Sometimes."

"I see. Well, I'm not drunk. Just trying to decide if I want to stay here."

"Oh. You got a reservation?"

Did the kid ever stop asking questions? A memory formed, that of his son, Elijah, at the same age. "Yeah, I do."

"Then why don't you wanna stay?"

Dominic glanced at the clock and noted the time. If he left now, he'd add another six hours to his drive from Atlanta. Not how he wanted to spend what was left of the day. Maybe he should spend the night and head back to Atlanta first thing in the morning? "You've convinced me. I guess I will stay."

"I'll show you the way to the office."

"Do your parents know you're out here near the street? You're awfully young to be wandering about on your own."

The kid's shoulders squared and he lifted his chin to a defiant angle.

"I'm almost ten."

He looked younger, maybe because of his small stature. "Well, almost ten or not, there are a lot of strangers milling around, and it's not safe for kids these days. Are you visiting?" He sounded like an old man talking about "the good old days" but it was true. What kind of parent just let their kid wander the streets in a beach town full of people, some of whom probably waited on the opportunity to grab a kid and head out of town?

"No. I live here. You coming or not?"

The kid had spunk, Dominic had to give him that.

He rolled up the windows of the Porsche 911, killing the powerful engine with another press of a button. He felt a little conspicuous driving the flashy car, but he had to admit he loved the power. Just like Lisa knew he would.

He opened the door and climbed out of the low vehicle, yet another thing to get used to after driving a family-friendly SUV for so many years.

"Wow. You're tall. My mom is too. I hope I'm tall when I grow up."

Dominic locked the car and fell into step behind

the boy. "I see the sign for the office. You can head home if you like."

"No. I need to check in anyway." The kid turned around and walked backward, rolling his eyes in classic kid fashion. "Or my mom will freak out and call the police again."

Again? "Does that happen a lot?"

"Her calling the police or freaking out?"

"Take your pick."

"Yeah."

Yeah to... both? Dom bit back another chuckle. Given the kid's intrepid personality, he probably kept his mom busy.

The kid flipped face-forward and Dom watched as the boy ran up the two steps leading to the office. He yanked open the door.

"Mom! Reservation!"

Dom noted the wide southern porch with its rocking chairs and a few chairs and tables before he followed the kid inside, well able to see why Lisa had liked the inn so much if the porch and office interior were anything by which to judge. It was her style of decorating. Beachy but understated.

The office walls were a soft gray with blue and sand-colored accents. There was a comfortable-looking couch and chair in the waiting area, a rope swing hanging from the ceiling in front of a painted mural of the beach and ocean behind, and on the opposite side, a coffee bar, popcorn machine, and snack area with a couple of parlor-type tables and chairs.

"Mom!"

"Samuel, how many times have I told you? No yelling. Inside voice," a woman stated as she appeared from a hallway behind the chest-high desk.

Dominic stilled, uncomfortable with the stomach-punching fact he found her beautiful. He'd guess her age to be early to mid-thirties, tall like her son said, at around five eight. Her auburn hair was scooped back and held at her nape, but curly tendrils framed her face and highlighted striking eyes that matched the blue of the ocean painting behind the check-in area.

"But, Mom, you have a reservation and sometimes don't hear me."

"A— Oh," she said, locking gazes with Dominic. "Sorry about that. Welcome to Carolina Cove Inn. I'm Ireland Cohen, the manager."

He forced himself to focus on her name rather than her beauty. "Ireland? Like the country?"

"Yes."

"Unusual name."

"Unusual family," she said by way of explanation. She flashed them both a smile. "I hope I didn't keep you waiting too long?"

"Not at all. Samuel kept me company."

"Mom, you should see his cool car! I'll bet it goes really fast. Does it?"

"It does."

"Maybe you'll take me for a ride sometime?"

"*Samuel.*"

"I'm leaving tomorrow."

"Oh."

"And even if he wasn't, Samuel, that's not something you ask our guests. We've talked about this, remember?" the boy's mother said while sliding her son a stern glare.

"Yes, ma'am."

Samuel glanced at Dominic and rolled his eyes, and yet again Dom found himself stifling a chuckle. And wondering at the last time he'd laughed so much in such a short span of time. "Tough break, kid."

"Let's get you checked in. Name?"

"Dominic Dunn."

"Domin—"

His name ended with a gasp and Ireland's eyes

filled with tears. She blinked rapidly and managed to keep them from falling, but in that instant, he knew she recognized him—and knew his reason for being there.

CLICK THE LAST GOODBYE TO KEEP READING!

- THE NANNY'S SECRET
- SOMEONE TO TRUST

THE STONE RIVER SERIES:

- WORTH THE WAIT
- NOT BY SIGHT
- THROUGH THE VALLEY
- LEAD ME NOT
- CHRISTMAS AT HOLLY WOOD
- THEIR CHRISTMAS MIRACLE
- SECOND CHANCES

SMALL TOWN SCANDALS SERIES:

- BRODY'S REDEMPTION
- FALLING FOR HER BOSS
- WITH THIS MAN

SECRET SANTA SERIES:

- SECRET SANTA
- SECRET SANTA II: A CHRISTMAS
  TO REMEMBER

MAKE ME A MATCH SERIES:

- ROMANCE RESET
- RULES OF ENGAGEMENT
- THE MATCHMAKER'S SECRET
- PERFECTLY MISMATCHED
- BY THE BOOK

CAROLINA COVE SERIES:

- SEASCAPES AND VEGAS MISTAKES
- SEASHELLS AND WEDDING BELLS
- SEA GLASS AND SECOND CHANCES
- SEA BLUE AND LOVING YOU
- SEA VIEW AND SOMETHING NEW

COMING SOON: (LINKS WILL BE UPDATED ASAP)

THE BLACKWELL BROTHERS SERIES:

- BABY BE MINE
- SECOND CHANCE WEDDING
- THE GETAWAY GUY

- OFF-LIMITS LOVE
- FLIRTING WITH FOREVER

ABOUT THE AUTHOR

Kay Lyons always wanted to be a writer, ever since the age of seven or eight when she copied the pictures out of a Charlie Brown book and rewrote the story because she didn't like the plot. Through the years her stories have changed but one characteristic stayed true— they were all romances. Each and every one of her manuscripts included a love story.

Published in 2005 with Harlequin Enterprises, Kay's first release was a national bestseller. Kay has also been a HOLT Medallion, Book Buyers Best and RITA Award nominee. Look for her most recent novels with Kindred Spirits Publishing.

For more information regarding her work, please visit Kay at the following:

www.kaylyonsauthor.com

@KayLyonsAuthor (Twitter)

Kay Lyons Author (Facebook)

Author_Kay_Lyons (Instagram)

Kay Lyons, Author (Pinterest)

FAQ ABOUT CAROLINA COVE:

Is Carolina Cove a real place?

Carolina Cove is purely fictional; however, it is **loosely** based on one of my favorite places—Kure Beach, North Carolina. Kure Beach is home to a wonderful pier, a pavilion for special events like weddings and birthdays, swings facing the Atlantic, pelicans Pete and George, coffee shops, restaurants, and more. It's also close to the North Carolina Aquarium, Carolina Beach, and Wilmington.

Can I stay at the Carolina Cove Inn?

While Carolina Cove and the Carolina Cove Inn are purely fictional, there are plenty of motels and rentals in the area to enjoy. One of my favorites is the Admirals Quarters. If you go, tell them Kay sent you! :)

The pier is real?

Yes! And it has quite a history. Be sure to check out the Kure Beach Pier Cam for a view of Kure Beach and the Atlantic.

What about the restaurants and coffee shops and places you've mentioned in the series?

London's Lattes is based on two of my favorite local coffee shops in Kure Beach and Carolina Beach. Are there more? Yes, plenty. But those two shops I know well because I've visited fairly often while writing these stories. Neither of them on their own was perfect for what I had in mind for London's, however, so I basically combined the two and ta-da! London's Lattes was born. But, no, if you go into either of them, you won't find London's exact business. Isn't fiction wonderful?

Why make up a city? Why not use Kure Beach?

One of the best things about writing fiction is that when a story appears a certain way, you can write it just that way. Carolina Cove and the characters appeared to me in story form and while Kure

Beach IS one of my favorite places, I had to change some things to better fit the series as well as steer far away from any real-life persons/families for obvious reasons. Doing so, that meant also changing the name of the city, etc. But, that said, you will find a slew of similarities in the fictional city and the real one. :)

Where is the dream catcher mailbox?

Unfortunately the dream catcher mailbox is pure fiction and an idea taken from a "beach mailbox" I visited once many years ago. The dream catcher mailbox first appeared in the SEASIDE SISTERS SERIES.

Update: I have been told a mailbox has been placed at the southern end of Ft. Fisher but I cannot confirm this.

How did you research the matchmaking aspect?

Oh, the answer to this was fun! Wilmington actually has a professional matchmaker. I interviewed her to get my details straight and learned a lot about a very fascinating business!

MAKE ME A MATCH SERIES:

- ROMANCE RESET
- RULES OF ENGAGEMENT
- THE MATCHMAKER'S SECRET
- PERFECTLY MISMATCHED
- BY THE BOOK

THE SEASIDE SISTERS SERIES:

- THE LAST GOODBYE
- LATTES AND LULLABYES
- MAP OF DREAMS
- WORTH THE RISK
- LOST LOVE FOUND

CAROLINA COVE SERIES:

- SEASCAPES AND VEGAS MISTAKES
- SEASHELLS AND WEDDING BELLS
- SEA GLASS AND SECOND CHANCES
- SEA BLUE AND LOVING YOU

COMING SOON: (LINKS WILL BE UPDATED ASAP)
THE BLACKWELL BROTHERS SERIES:

- BABY BE MINE
- SECOND CHANCE WEDDING
- THE GETAWAY GUY
- OFF-LIMITS LOVE
- FLIRTING WITH FOREVER